Gerhard Roth

There Is No Evil Angel But Love

A Novel

Gerhard Roth

There Is No Evil Angel But Love

A Novel

Translated and with an Afterword
by Todd C. Hanlin

Ariadne Press
Riverside, CA

There Is No Evil Angel But Love
By Gerhard Roth

Translated and with an Afterword
by Todd C. Hanlin
reprinted with kind permission by the author
© 2022 Todd C. Hanlin

Gerhard Roth: *Es gibt keinen böseren Engel als die Liebe*
© S. Fischer Verlag GmbH, Frankfurt am Main, 2021.
All rights reserved by S. Fischer Verlag GmbH.
(ISBN 978-3-10-397214-6)

Front cover photo © Ghouston, via Wikimedia Commons
Image credits, in order of appearance:
P. 41. Winsor McCay: *Little Nemo in Slumberland*, book edition.
P. 56. Image from Jodorowsky/Moebius: *The Incal*, Vol. 1.
    © 2020 Humanoids, Inc., Los Angeles.
Pp. 120–121. Guggenheim Museum, Venice.
    Photos: © Gerhard Roth.
P. 134. Maria Lassnig, *Du oder Ich* (You or Me), 2005
    © Maria Lassnig Foundation
    Photo: Stefan Altenburger Photography Zurich
P. 137. Rosalba Carriera: *Young Lady of the Le Blond Family*,
    Gallerie dell'Accademia, Venice.
P. 137. Giorgione: *The Tempest*, Gallerie dell' Accademia, Venice.
P. 141. Walter Sickert: *San Marco, Venice*.
Pp. 152–153. Giovanni Domenico Tiepolo: *Il Mondo Novo*,
    fresco from the Villa Zianigo, Ca' Rezzonico, Venice.
P. 157. Pietro Longhi: *The Rhinoceros*, 1751, Ca' Rezzonico, Venice.
P. 163. Samurai armor in the Museo d'Arte Orientale, Venice.
    Photo: © Gerhard Roth.

Publisher's Cataloging-in-Publication data

Names: Roth, Gerhard, 1942 June 24-2022, author. | Hanlin, Todd C.,
translator.
Title: There is no evil angel but love : a novel / Gerhard Roth; translated
and with an afterword by Todd C. Hanlin.
Description: Riverside, CA: Ariadne Press, 2023.
Identifiers: LCCN: 2023920267 | ISBN: 978-1-57241-233-0 (paperback)
| 978-1-57241-230-9 (ebook)
Subjects: LCSH Widows--Fiction. | Art historians--Fiction. | BISAC
FICTION / World Literature / Austria / 21st Century
Classification: LCC PT2678.O79615 T44 2023 | DDC 813.6--dc23

There ain't no answer.
There ain't gonna be any answer.
There never has been an answer.
That's the answer.

Gertrude Stein
Brewsie and Willie

1

The Burial of Klemens Kuck
and Lilli's Flight from Reality

"The first thing I learned about my father was the occasion when the Pope washed his feet," Lilli read. She simply couldn't read any more of her husband's childhood memories, composed in mirror writing, because she couldn't keep her eyes open.

Since Klemens' death, Lilli had been taking sedatives and sleeping pills to be able to bear the pain, the sorrow, and the certainty of never seeing him again. Klemens had fallen over a bridge walkway in Venice and been transported to Vienna where he died two weeks later in intensive care without regaining consciousness. Everything about his death had been puzzling. Although he had been in the Italian city for four weeks, he hadn't been registered in any hotel or pension, so the police concluded that he must have been staying privately. That was strange, because he had phoned her every day and claimed that he was staying at the Hotel Diana near St. Mark's Square. Of course, now she was afraid that he might have been cheating on her, but there was no indication that was the case.

On the morning of his funeral, she woke up with a desire to travel to Venice herself. Shortly afterward, she received an envelope with Klemens' black notebook and the drawings he had made in Venice—from a certain Guido Alberti, though without a return address. She packed a suitcase, informed her superior in the Kunsthistorisches Museum that she was taking three weeks' leave, dressed in black, and drove her three-year-old Volvo to the Central Cemetery where Klemens was buried in a grave of honor from the city of Vienna. Acting on impulse, she didn't make an appearance at the funeral banquet following the ceremony, but had her sister apologize for her absence. The solemnities were hard for her to bear.

Klemens had illustrated and written comic books, and had become a sensation in recent years. For that reason, other artists, journalists, television reporters, colleagues from the Kunsthistorisches Museum, as well as countless young people and curiosity seekers, along with—in accordance with his oft-repeated wish—five musicians from the State Opera who played the second movement of the Schubert *Quintet* before the casket disappeared into the grave.

After Lilli had gotten behind the wheel, she opened one of the two notebooks with Klemens' childhood memories and drawings that she had put on the passenger's seat that morning, and took out the slip of paper where he had noted: "My mother, Maria Pichlmayer, Hallstatt Landing, 'Inn of the Ice Saints,'" and, below that, a mailing address and telephone number.

She first set out for Upper Austria and Salzburg, then pulled over at a rest area to telephone.

Her brain was full of jumbled images that were mixed with the passing landscape and the road surface: the white casket, floral wreaths, familiar and unfamiliar faces, the musicians who played with serious expressions, and the eulogists who had no idea who Klemens had really been. She, herself, didn't even know. When she thought about him, she recalled the scenes when he was inspired by things he had just seen. He had scribbled countless notebooks full of sketches: beginning with patterns on butterfly wings or Oriental carpets, pictures in museums or children's drawings, and graduating to cloud and leaf formations, snowflakes, and even junk—one of his favorites. He recorded everything quickly and precisely—he captured people's faces as easily as the appearance of animals. He drew on trains, in coffeehouses and hotel rooms, even out on the street, in churches or parking lots. He realized beauty as well as the ridiculous, tragedy as well as comedy.

After she had dialed the telephone number on Klemens' slip of paper, a woman's voice answered and confirmed that Frau Pichlmayer was there. Without another word, Lilli ended the call and drove on.

The highway now seemed like a movie that was playing before her, and her memories were superimposed on top of it in high-key lighting. Later, she only saw the roadway fragmentally.

She parked the Volvo at a parking area above Hallstatt and just sat in the car for a while. Her husband had never mentioned that his mother (who had given him up for adoption at birth) lived here. He had also not told Lilli how and when he had acquired his mother's address.

She took several deep breaths until the picture of his face dissolved in her mind. The view of Lake Hallstatt and the old houses were, for her, like windows onto the past.

The Inn of the Ice Saints was directly on the lake, as a light breeze ruffled the water's surface. The Mill Pond near the Alster in Hamburg came to mind, along with the bright summer days that she had spent roller-skating as a child and adolescent.

She asked a waiter in the elegant hotel for Frau Pichlmayer. The place was furnished in a rustic and expensive style, but since it was still early evening, she quickly found a table by a window with a view of sailboats and an excursion ship reflected in the dazzling water. Absolutely everything in Hallstatt was picturesque. The glacier lake between the high mountains looked like a fjord, and although the lake seemed peaceful, she knew that storms could create waves that capsized sailboats. She had read that it was more than 400-feet deep, and some drowning victims had never been recovered. Instantly her thoughts were back at her husband's burial. The Schubert *Quintet* had moved her, as if someone had spoken to her who knew all the sorrows of the world.

At that moment, an elderly lady, expensively dressed and

wearing a white tunic, appeared at her table. Lilli was convinced that this was the woman she was looking for, so she stood up, introduced herself, and informed the lady that her son had been buried in Vienna that morning.

"Klemens?" the lady asked. She turned and fled to the outdoor dining area where she sat down at a corner table far from the entrance.

She just stared at the tabletop.

"My husband doesn't know about Klemens," she said to the tabletop. She then raised her head and looked at Lilli warily with teary eyes.

"What do you want from me?" she asked.

"Who is his father?" Lilli replied earnestly.

"Klemens asked me that very same question . . ."

"I didn't know that."

"He was here more than a month ago, and I told him the name." She cleared her throat and added: "His name is Galli and he's a policeman, an inspector in Venice, I think."

"Do you have his address?" Lilli asked.

"He insisted that he came from Padua. Later, it turned out that he was living in Venice."

"Would you please tell me his first name?"

"Francesco . . . I don't want to have anything to do with him." She looked off to one side, and, after a brief pause, asked: "What happened to Klemens?"

Lilli told her of the accident and realized that Klemens' mother knew nothing about her son. She only read the newspaper once in a while, she insisted, and she also wasn't interested in the news on TV.

Lilli heard footsteps on the gravel, and when she looked up, Frau Pichlmayer whispered anxiously: "My husband!"

A moment later he was standing before them, snorting angrily: "There you are!"

When Lilli saw him, she instantly thought of a white kitchen clock. He had a bloated face, a bald head, an apron around his belly, and a white toque on his head. It really could just be a living kitchen clock with a wind-up key on top, Lilli fantasized. His face twitched, as if it wanted to reveal that he hated the world.

"The lady and I are discussing a wedding."

"When is it supposed to be?" he asked suspiciously.

"In September."

"We're at capacity in September," the giant kitchen clock responded with a scowl, putting an end to the conversation. He bustled off, disgruntled, turning back one more time and spitting out: "You ought to know that!"

Frau Pichlmayer was silent until he had disappeared. In the meantime, the word "wedding" had incidentally reminded Lilli of Klemens' burial. She stood up, as if according to protocol, and went to her car without a backward glance. The whole time she thought about fleeing, but she couldn't think of a place where she wanted to go. She mechanically got into her car and drove off in the direction of Italy, without knowing if she really wanted to go there. In any event, not back to Vienna, and not to Hamburg either, where she had spent her childhood and youth. It then occurred to her that Klemens had sometimes said: "He who does not know where he is going, will get the furthest."

"That sentiment is from Shakespeare," he had added . . .

2

Venice

She was already in Italy when she stopped for the night. She didn't care where she was, she was simply following her inner-navigator. Whenever they were on a road trip, Klemens would often fall asleep beside her and wake up only when they had arrived at their destination . . . It occurred to her that he was now beneath the ground, and she diverted herself by observing the scenery along the way. The sun was shining, elderberry bushes and acacia trees were in blossom, green parkways lined the highway, and crystal-flashing rivers left her with the impression that everything had been created just for her alone. But she still felt more alone than ever before in her entire life. She was suddenly overcome by a paralyzing feeling, like an unexpectedly thick fog.

Every time they had traveled to Venice, they had first gone through Jesolo: past the small pensions, the towering water slide, the brooks and front yards, until they reached the Punta Sabbioni and had then parked their car at one of the guarded parking lots behind the villas. This time, too, she paid the fee for the entirety of her intended stay.

While she was waiting for the passenger ship that would take her from Punta Sabbioni to St. Mark's Square, she called family members and her closest friends, briefly informing them that she was in Padua to view the Scrovegni Chapel with its frescoes by

Giotto. She thought it was a good idea to lie. She employed the same lie with each of her phone calls, and each time she was relieved by the thought of vanishing. The last thing she said was that she would call, but otherwise her phone would be turned off.

The ship, coming from Burano, finally docked, and as she dragged her suitcase on-board, she thought of all the things she had left behind, but that didn't bother her. Since Klemens' death, she felt horribly alone, but she told herself that was how everybody felt. Most of the passengers on board had probably experienced how hideous sorrow and pain were. When she decided to read the two notebooks about Klemens' childhood, she again remembered that he had drafted all of his books and notes in mirror writing and how arduous deciphering it would be. Klemens had enjoyed cloaking his work in a secret. Until his manuscripts were finished, he locked them in a safe, wrapped in newspapers with the tag: "Do not read!" Even though she had been curious, she had always obeyed this command. As soon as he had completed a comic book, she was always the first one who was allowed to see the pages and the illustrations. While reading, she was sometimes shocked to learn what was going on in his head.

As she looked out the window, she discovered paddle-boats in the distance. When the boaters flourished their paddles in the sun, the oar blades reflected the light so that she witnessed a continual blinking, as if from giant fireflies, even though it was broad daylight. As the steamer set off from Punta Sabbioni, the ship poured out thick black smoke that drifted over its roof in patches. She decided dispassionately that she, too, was dispersing and would eventually disappear. That was a bizarre consolation, combined with her spontaneous desire to never go home again. In her present condition, the first thing she couldn't stand was the familiar—only foreign things seemed to fit her mental state. People had told her that she was a strong woman, but it was hard enough to be a human being and vulnerable. At the same time, she realized that she had unintentionally spoken this last thought out loud, even if softly; she glanced around to see if anyone had noticed, but they all seemed lost in their own little worlds.

She noticed remnants of white tissues lying by a bench in the passenger cabin, and with the ship's movement, two empty soft drink bottles of transparent plastic rolled across the deck. She turned away and studied the other passengers: elderly women with full shopping bags stared off into space, and curious tourists strained to catch everything passing by the windows or they studied some description in a travel guide.

The steamer docked at the Santa Maria Elisabetta station on the Lido. Passengers got off, others came on-board, she had seen this all before, but it still seemed suddenly new—though she didn't know why. It reminded her of yet another feeling from her childhood when she had ridden home from school on the subway.

San Zaccaria was the end of the line, and the steamer would then turn around and sail back to Punta Sabbioni. She hadn't even inquired whether there was a room for her at the Hotel Pandora behind St. Mark's Square, but she trusted that the concierge would remember her, since she had stayed there several times with Klemens.

There were so many boats and vaporetti waiting at San Zaccaria that the steamer docked at the beginning of the Riva degli Schiavoni, so that Lilli had to drag her suitcase up and down four or five stone bridges. The way seemed endlessly long, and she was on the verge of tears. One lane on the bridges was provided with planks for invalids, baby carriages, and shopping carts. Nevertheless, she felt frazzled.

She finally sat down on a bench in the arcade of the Doge's Palace. A sweating man sat next to her, his eyes closed, as if he were sleeping. She briefly sized him up and gazed at St. Mark's; each time she had visited the square with Klemens, it had been an experience. But this time it was only a familiar sight, as if she would come here every day. A bit further on, the Basilica. The majority of tourists consider-ed it a museum. But every time they had visited, she recalled, Klemens had run up the steep stairway to the top floor, had sat down on a bench at the parapet, and stared at the golden mosaic cupola with its sacred figures. Immediately to the left was Hell, and Klemens had viewed the depiction again and again, each time photographing it all over again. He had also shot the cupola—especially the mosaic of the Creation—and the ornamentation of the ancient flooring.

She got up, took hold of her suitcase, and dragged it along behind her. It was so warm that she began to perspire.

Maybe it would be better not to stay at the Hotel Pandora, but at the Hotel Diana across the street, she thought, as she turned into the street where both hotels were located. The glass door of the Hotel Diana, where Klemens had apparently stayed on his last trip to Venice, was locked, as usual during midday . . . Guests had to enter a combination that was changed every day, or they could try to gain access via the Hotel Pandora that belonged to the same corporate entity.

Tourists with their luggage were backed up at the front desk, so she detoured to the nearby cramped lobby. Exhausted, she dropped into an armchair upholstered in a rose pattern where she waited until all the other guests had been checked in.

Eventually they were only able to find a room for her in the Hotel Diana. A tall Afro-European in a brown uniform with a gold sash and buttons followed her in double-time across the narrow road and brought her suitcase that she had left in the Hotel Pandora. Laughing, he explained that she could open the glass door at the hotel entrance with the combination 113E. They then entered the deserted building and rode the elevator up one floor without seeing a single soul. Once in the room, she was appalled. First of all, she noticed that the noise from the tourists in the crowded street down below was very loud. She looked up and saw the nearby exterior wall of the building across the way, its shutters closed. Her room, too, was strikingly cramped. But the ceiling was almost 15 feet high, and one of the walls was hidden behind a dark-brown 10-foot-tall monster wardrobe. She immediately thought of a coffin . . . When she tried to open the sliding door, it was stuck. Meanwhile, the tall English-speaking Afro-European had placed Lilli's suitcase beside the double bed with its red bedspread in a gold-checked pattern. He then inserted a plastic card in its intended slot, which turned on the lights. When Lilli tried to give him a tip, he surprised her by turning it down.

She laid down on the bed and closed her eyes.

She woke up half an hour later, when she heard knocking at her door. But she didn't want to speak with anyone. The knocking continued, but she stayed in bed, motionless, and just stared at the ceiling. When it was quiet again, she got up to put her clothes away in the wardrobe and almost stumbled over a suitcase. She now saw that it wasn't hers. She opened the unfamiliar luggage, looking for something to identify the owner, and discovered magic supplies: among other things, a skull, a deck of cards, a collapsible opera hat, and silk scarves. She closed the lid and tried to call someone from the hotel, but no one answered. She opened the suitcase once more and, to her amazement, stumbled onto a set of false teeth, pill packs with sedatives, painkillers, and sleeping pills, a pistol that she assumed was only for firing blanks, an asthma inhaler, and photographs. She felt as if she knew the man in the photographs. Like she herself, it was likely that he and his spouse had lived in the luxury condominium complex "Am Heumarkt" in the heart of Vienna before he disappeared from sight, she recalled. Only then did she remember that he had been a prompter at the Vienna State Opera.

"Disappeared," she sighed, as she spoke the word, because she felt an ever growing need to disappear or at least become invisible. Could there be some identification in the suitcase? Several photographs depicted the man—she now knew that his name was Aldrian—with an attractive woman, not the one she had known back then, but perhaps his lover or new wife. She then found photos that showed billboards, reading: IL GRANDE MAESTRO SUGGERITORE, which, as she knew, meant "The Great Master Prompter." He apparently performed these days as a magician. In a cardboard box she found a rabbit mask, a dog mask, and a bird mask, and as if she were drunk, she put them on, one after the other, and inspected herself in the tiny bathroom mirror. She had turned into a rabbit, a dog, and a bird, and could smile for the first time. Also in the suitcase was a blue star-studded theatrical costume . . . She slipped it on—why she did it, she later couldn't remember. It was much too big and hung loosely on her, which made her feel just like a child again. She had to leave the past behind, she told herself, and the thought consoled her in some mysterious way.

The blank pistol was heavy. It was possibly a real firearm—she also found a box with bullets. She finally took the sleeping pills and pain killers out of the suitcase, enough for a week. She didn't feel she was doing anything wrong, certainly nothing as concrete as "stealing." A glass chandelier hung from the ceiling—a polyp with eight tentacles, she thought, that glows in the ocean depths, or an electric flower vase with large radiant blossoms . . . Then she noticed the leaf-shaped glass wall lamps beside the bed, a gold-framed painting of pink and white roses hanging above it. She tried to phone the porter or a bellhop, but no one answered. So, she slipped on her shoes and requested a different room at the front desk of the Hotel Pandora across the street. The answer was the empty promise of *domani*. "Domani," tomorrow, was a word she had known since childhood, her father had always insisted it was the perpetual Italian calendar.

In her room, she unpacked her own suitcase, showered, took a sedative and a painkiller, and soon fell fast asleep.

3

A Little Mosaic Stone in St. Mark's Basilica

When she opened her eyes, she discovered that her headache was gone, which surprised her. The strange suitcase still lay there, open, on the floor. She was amazed at the coincidence that had brought it to her of all people. If that had any significance, then what would it be?

Since she had brought her iPad along, she connected it to the Wi-Fi network, typed in passwords until everything was functioning properly, and then turned once again to the strange suitcase. There was also a musical score among the scattered items, it was Rossini's *Thieving Magpie*. That was a further indication that the suitcase must belong to the former prompter Aldrian. First, she went into the bathroom and subsequently to the breakfast room that was separated from the lobby by a wooden partition.

After she had eaten some small white pastries and a soft-boiled egg, butter, marmalade and cream cheese, while thinking of Klemens, she looked for the porter (who recognized her after a brief hesitation). He asked if he could be of assistance. Lilli automatically requested different accommodations, she couldn't stand being in that cramped room. The porter rushed to the computer to check, and explained that, at the moment, there was only a vacant room on the third floor where the street noise would be less loud, or—after tomorrow, "domani"—the room she and her husband had previously booked many times, with windows overlooking the courtyard. She decided to wait until the next day, and then mentioned the suitcase that had been placed in her room by mistake. The porter promised that he would look into it immediately, and Lilli took the elevator back to her "disgusting coffin room," as she had called it from the outset. Once there, she reached into her bag and took out the black notebook that some fellow named Guido Alberti had sent without a return address, in which Klemens had made notes and sketches in mirror writing about his last stay in Venice. But she stuffed it back into her duffel bag and decided to read it in Caffé Florian. In any case, she hoped it might give her a clue to the puzzling events that had led to his death. And she wanted to be close to him, as well.

She only had to walk down the narrow street, turn the corner twice, and she was at St. Mark's Square that was swamped by highwater and whose buildings were reflected on the water's surface. Tourists stood at the periphery and were taking pictures of the laughing people who had taken off their shoes and rolled up their jeans.

Acting on impulse, Lilli took off her sandals and stepped into the cold water without displaying any reaction. Klemens would have most certainly encouraged her, she thought. "And what now?" she asked him silently. "What should I do now?" He was silent.

With her sandals in hand, she simply let the crowd take her to the Basilica atrium where she watched workers in orange-colored overalls sweep water out of the Basilica. "Don't ask anyone!" she heard Klemens in her head, the way he usually impelled his audacious stunts when obstacles had to be overcome. She heard two workers shouting and pointing, but, ignoring them, she hurried up the steep stairway behind the entrance, sandals still in hand. The water covered the designs of the stone flooring like a giant magnifying glass, and Lilli imagined that the men were sweeping the now-liquid designs out of the Basilica. Streaks of light flitted across the mosaic walls in a flash, and then were gone. She reached the gallery on the top floor where she could once again view the golden mosaic cupolas and walls. At that point she slipped back into her sandals.

As seen from above, the full magnificence was reflected on the water, and it seemed to Lilli as if she had arrived at a parallel universe. Klemens had especially admired the cupola of the creation—the Genesis Cupola—with its images over the atrium. In the first scene, Lilli knew, the spirit of God hovered over the waters in the form of a white dove, the Creator then separated light and darkness, and created the firmament and plants. The second narrative scene depicted the creation of the planets, birds, inhabitants of the oceans, terrestrial animals, and the first human being, Adam. In the third and final scene, Adam gave names to the animals, Eve was created and led by God to Adam in Paradise. Finally, Eve succumbed to temptation and received from Satan in the form of a snake the fruit of the tree of knowledge that she gave to Adam and ate with him, causing their "fall from grace." Adam and Eve tried to hide from God, but He saw them, first cursed the snake Satan and then had the Archangel Michael expel them from Paradise. In the final picture, Adam was chopping wood and Eve was spinning flax. The adjacent wall surface portrayed the births of their children—Cain and Abel—their offerings to God, and, last of all, above the entrance to the Zen chapel, Cain's murder of Abel. For Klemens, the entire history of mankind was captured in the golden mosaics, or, as he would say, its DNA. Most of all, Klemens liked to look at the Noah Chapel, from the building of the ark to the flood, from the return of the dove with an olive branch in its beak to Noah's burial. Directly across from it was the Tower of Babel in a childish rendition and, to one side, the Babylonian confusion of tongues.

On one visit, Lilli remembered, Klemens had spent a great deal of time studying the mosaic of Jesus washing the feet of the twelve apostles, which made her think of Klemens' drawings of the Pope washing his father's feet.

The main part of the Basilica was devoted to the life and persecution of Jesus and his murder by human hands. Klemens had framed that as "the basic explanation of humanity," we destroyed our life in Paradise and, in the end, killed the Creator of the universe. However, each time Klemens emphasized that God had created man and Lucifer in His own image.

Even though she had become familiar with St. Mark's Basilica with its cupolas and alcoves as a child and later during her university years, it was Klemens who had first pointed out the depiction of the Day of Judgment that was never reproduced nor mentioned in any of her books.

She stood up, glanced up at the mosaics above her, and calmly came to the conclusion that she was insignificant. She had the feeling that she was in the brain of the Basilica and was studying its stone memories. What would archeologists deduce from the mosaics, Lilli asked herself, if there were no further explanations for these pictures? . . . It was comforting that, in the Basilica, there was no such thing as time, even when the bells rang, they were only acoustical embellishments, she told herself. The gold all around her wasn't sparkling or glowing, but was rather mysteriously dark, a gold—as she described it—that was sleeping and dreaming mosaics. It seemed as if she were gazing into a world after death. The mosaics now silently began to move and to take life in her mind.

She found the floor of colorful marble chips—the stone carpet, as she called it—just as attractive as the mosaics, except they remained motionless (when they weren't covered by water) as if they were single frames at different moments of time. Then, again, she thought of the sleeping mind of some fantastic creature, full of visions and dreams. And she had the impression that there was something inside her that she still had to discover.

In the mosaic of the Judgement Day—immediately beside the bench where she was sitting—there were grey bundles of clouds, with God, the saints and angels, hovering above—close together, like in the painting of *Paradise* by Tintoretto in the Doge's Palace—while those condemned to Hell were herded together on a grotesquely huge devil's tail, driven, like cattle, into the dark by angels with lances and swords, and tossed on top of each other into the inferno.

The faces of the sinners expressed fear, pain, resignation, and torment.

It wasn't just that Lilli was near the Judgment Day in this gallery, she could even touch the mosaic stones—the little gold plates, black and white chips—and thus realise the artwork's atomic structure. Each time she was amazed at how small the little stones were. From the pointillist painting style of a Georges Seurat or Paul Signac, she understood the similar fine-pointed stone composition. This was perhaps the greatest experience she received from the Basilica: the origin of an occurrence from the tiniest of details. Behind her was a plexiglass roof, and she could look through it, down to the atrium where little men in orange-colored overalls were still sweeping water out of the Basilica. Later, tourists would move through the building like ants on their well-worn trail. As she inadvertently glanced down at the floor, she discovered a small mosaic stone, a glass chip, overlaid with gold leaf that must have come loose from the wall. She quickly bent down, picked it up, and, without a second thought, put it in the pocket of her jeans. She immediately began to search for the spot where it belonged and discovered that it was the gold stone from above the head of an angel who was threatening the damned with his lance. It was clear that the gold background of the mosaics was an expression of light which, in the Middle Ages, was God Himself. Not far from that, over Paradise, she also discovered the seven-headed dragon. As she knew, it depicted a citation from the Book of Revelation where Satan is described as a dragon, "great, fiery red dragon having seven heads and ten horns, and seven diadems on his heads." With that, she thought about the little mosaic stone in her pocket. Should she keep it?

"Signora!" a voice called out. Since she didn't under-stand Italian, the man in orange overalls spoke to her in broken English, out of breath from climbing the stairs, as he approached: "You must go . . . Scusi."

Lilli again thought about the little mosaic stone and followed the worker in overalls as he hurried down the stairs. While he was apologizing once more, she left the Basilica, relieved.

St. Mark's Square was still covered in water, and the tourists were still taking pictures of each other. A low-flying pigeon grazed her head with one wing, which seemed to her like a mystical experience. Involuntarily—sandals still in her hand—Lilli crossed the Square and heard the two music bands, one in front of Caffè Florian, the other in front of Gran Caffè Quadri. She was relieved that she hadn't gotten into trouble with the little mosaic stone. She felt as if she were crossing a river and setting foot in a new country. Caffè Florian was wonderful terrain, a compilation of memories and the present. While the band in front of Gran Caffè Quadri played Wagner in the style of an operetta overture, the ensemble at Caffè Florian gave renditions of Verdi arias and folksongs. After slipping into her sandals, she automatically entered the establishment and saw Roberto, the head waiter, in his usual white shirt and jacket. And he recognized her, waved to her, hurried over and asked how Klemens was. People were saying that he had had an accident and had fallen over the balustrade on the Ponte degli Scalzi near the main train station.

"He's dead," Lilli answered. "He was buried yesterday."

Roberto gasped and turned aside. *"Mie condoglianze*—my condolences," he said, stunned.

"He was pushed down the stairs by someone, and I will find the person who did it."

She thought again of the golden little mosaic stone in her pants pocket and was amazed that she had told Roberto that Klemens had been pushed down the stairs and that she would find the person who did it. She didn't really know that someone had pushed him, and, until now, hadn't really had the intention of finding the culprit.

Roberto nodded, hurried ahead of her through the busy rooms, and led her to the table where she had usually sat with Klemens. She glanced at the pictures on the wall which apparently had something to do with the Biennale—projection screens, weighted with wooden rods, were rolled-down to show new projections that overlaid the previous ones. Opposite the window was a larger-than-life angel, operating a Morse telegraph with one hand and perforated strips of paper curled at its feet. In the other hand it held a triangle. To its left, a small cherubic head, tiny ships in the background. Lilli liked the picture. It combined technology and religion in a magical-satirical way. She ordered a chocolate torte and a *Spritz*, made with Prosecco, Aperol, and soda water that had been Klemens' favorite drink.

Before she began to read the notebook about his last stay in Venice, she glanced through the large window and out onto St. Mark's Square. The *acqua alta* didn't seem as deep, but even more visitors than before were standing in the water, some with outstretched arms and open hands, feeding pigeons that landed on their heads and shoulders, then flew up and landed again. When she had first come to St. Mark's Square as a child, she recalled, she couldn't get enough of the pigeons. She now thought so intensively about her past that she imagined reliving her thoughts and feelings back then. She then began to decipher the black notebook that was drafted in mirror writing. Klemens had evidently scribbled everything down in a great hurry, at any rate her reading didn't progress beyond spelling words out in a tedious mute process. So, she asked Roberto for some paper and began to copy down the pages.

She was occupied with Klemens' entries until it got dark. It was clear to her that she would retrace the routes and stops that were described in the notebooks. She had already emptied her sixth glass of Spritz and eaten another piece of the chocolate torte. And, except for two large puddles, the *acqua alta* on the Square had almost completely disappeared. Without wasting a word on his reason or purpose, Klemens had described trips from Venice to Padua, Pellestrina, Chioggia, Sant'Erasmo, and to the monastery island of San Lazzaro degli Armeni, in addition to several visits to museums and exhibitions. It was up to her to find some continuity. Where had Klemens been living? Had he had a lover? Who was Guido Alberti, the man who had sent her the black notebook? And why had Klemens twice visited an *asilo* in Cannaregio?

She paid her bill and spoke with the headwaiter, asking who had been with Klemens on his visits to Caffè Florian . . . Had it been a woman? A man? Roberto shook his head. He wasn't at the Caffè at all hours of the day and night, so he would ask his colleagues for further information: Yes, there had been a woman, two or three times, he had seen that himself, a Japanese woman who had spoken with "Signor Kuck" for a long time. And every once in a while, he had been accompanied by a furniture dealer who was apparently a good friend.

"Guido Alberti?" she asked.

"Yes, Alberti!" In a day or two he could perhaps provide her with more names and addresses. On impulse, Lilli didn't mention to him that Alberti had sent her Klemens' notes.

As she walked over to the Basilica, she felt that she had eaten too little and drunk too much. She staggered, but at that moment, someone took her by the elbow and helped her regain her balance. Without a word of thanks, she hurried off, bought a city map of Venice, and took the elevator up to her room. She told herself that she had become confused from the exhausting work of deciphering the mirror writing. Instead of ordering a meal from room service, she sat at the window with the map and stared out at the hubbub before her. She remembered Roberto also mentioning that Klemens, slovenly dressed, had followed various strangers into the Caffè, would sit down anyplace, order a glass of mineral water, and open a newspaper. Apparently, he would just wait for the stranger to leave, and he would abruptly follow him. There was talk that he was planning something shady.

When she looked around the ugly hotel room, she discovered that the suitcase with the magic items was still in its old place . . . and the room itself had turned into an elevator cabin that continually went up and down.

4

A Murder and an Interrogation

Lilli woke at sunrise with a headache, nausea, and dizziness. She swore that that was her last night in the "coffin room." The mirror writing from Klemens' notes were rumbling around in her head and automatically formed reversed words before her very eyes. Klemens had been left-handed and could write out a text in mirror writing in both the right and left hands simultaneously. He had told her time and time again that Leonardo da Vinci had written his personal notes only in mirror writing. The brain, he explained, was a labyrinth, actually a double-maze, as a result of its two halves that were built "symmetrically identical." He even knew that it was equipped with two different locomotor systems. One served minor movements, such as writing; the other, movements of the body, like walking. This "movement center" had to continuously carry out "mirror movements" on a daily basis. There were special nerve cells in the brain devoted to movement, the "mirror neurons." They influenced empathy and recognition of actions. Klemens couldn't say enough about it. On the other hand, he would continue, laughing, there were also "anti-mirror neurons" that played a significant role in observation. The brain's entire mirror system had been studied in monkeys, specifically their observation of human activities and their resulting imitations. In a similar fashion, the human brain provides predictions of the "unexpected" and even of the "forthcoming."

She swallowed a pain pill that she had taken from the magic suitcase and ordered breakfast from room service. By the time it reached her table, she forced herself to eat everything, hoping to get rid of the dizziness in her head: fried eggs, white bread, ham, marmalade, and she alternately drank coffee and mineral water. She then lay back down on the bed and telephoned the porter. She insisted on the promised "other" room and complained that the stranger's suitcase had still not been retrieved. The porter apologized and explained in a sad voice that everything was being taken care of. She could move into room number 42 on the next floor, her suitcase would be brought to her new room.

As it turned out, it really was the room that she and Klemens had enjoyed: a large airy room with a double bed, relatively quiet, with a view of two garden restaurants in the rear courtyard. Gold-framed pictures hung between the two windows and above the bed. She took the small mosaic stone out of her pants pocket and put it on the night stand. Deep down, she felt that it protected her. It was unique, she was sure of that. However, her purse was not the place to keep it, because loose change would break it, she told herself. In the end, she took her sunglasses out of their leather case and stored it in there. From now on, she would always carry it with her, because the small glass chip seemed to her like a fragment from Klemens' universe of ideas.

She was very familiar with the usual pictures on the walls of the hotel room. Of course, they were kitsch: a young shepherd playing a flute, with an equally young shepherdess, a basket of fruit with grapes, peaches, and plums.

The furniture was white and the chandelier on the ceiling the same model as in the first room, but it had a different effect due to the light and the ambiance. Besides, she knew that she could look down on the open-air restaurants below and hear their chatter during the summer months. Outside, there were blue skies and sunshine. She gradually felt that she was doing better, and the desire to be outdoors virtually overwhelmed her.

She thought again about Guido Alberti, and she decided to locate him.

She would later have an indelible picture in her head of exactly what happened next.

First, she strolled beneath the arcades in St. Mark's Square, heading in the direction of the Museo Correr. It was sunny, but cool in the shade. She remembered the display windows of the jewelers, the glass and stationery stores . . . They had stayed twice near the Bacino Orseolo, in the Albergo Cavaletto, her favorite hotel by far. It was directly behind St. Mark's Square on a kind of small harbor that had been built two hundred years ago to create a dock for gondolas in the middle of the city. From their rooms, they could gaze directly at the countless black boats and into the surrounding buildings of one of the most elegant clothing stores or visit the modern Hard Rock Café. The street was the Calle del Salvadego, as best she could remember.

She turned off to the right after a glass studio that was across from a mask shop. In the front window she saw masks of a lion, an elephant, a dog, a zebra, a rhinoceros, and an ape. It occurred to her that there were also animal masks in the magic suitcase that had landed in her room.

A few steps further on, she noticed another glass studio featuring a small she-devil and an equally small devil, cats, but also a horse. In the midst of the welter of figures, she inadvertently spotted Death, and hurried on. A Hugo Boss store and its display window with male mannequins in suits was followed by an insurance company.

When she reached the Bacino, she discovered more gondolas than she had ever seen before. A group of Japanese, older women with large hats, were waiting on the walkway at the dock. Behind them, the famous Hotel Cavaletto & Doge Orseolo, and she even knew from which windows she and Klemens had watched the activity in the Bacino. In the hotel restaurant and bar, you sat almost at the water level. Even back then, Klemens had eagerly taken notes . . . Meanwhile, Lilli had sat down on a plastic crate and noticed that one of the Japanese women was waving to her. It reminded her of Roberto's remark, that Klemens had visited Caffè Florian several times in the company of a Japanese woman. From one moment to the next, she stood up and walked back to the Caffè.

The "small orchestra," as Klemens had always called it, laughingly, was just playing "Happy Birthday" for a party; there was enthusiastic applause, and the band then took a break. Each of the musicians had a music stand. As she got closer, she saw the pianist at the black piano. A young lady was playing a violin, and two older gentlemen were playing a double bass and a harmonica. She sat down outside and, in spite of her intention to avoid alcohol, ordered a Campari. She then got the city map out of her duffel bag, along with the notes she had copied yesterday from Klemens' black notebook, and began to trace on the map the routes he had taken. As best she could recall, from this point on, she later only saw her lines and asterisks in the street labyrinth on the map.

Roberto was on duty that afternoon and, just after starting work, he hurried over to her and hastily reported that Klemens had really led two lives. After he had apparently followed somebody while wearing scruffy outfits, he would then appear in his best clothes in the company of men or women—frequently with the Japanese woman—and would leave generous tips.

"When he was working intensely," Lilli interrupted, "he didn't pay much attention to what he was wearing."

With that, the head waiter disappeared discreetly, only to reappear fifteen minutes later and to apologize. But, again, Robert looked to one side, bowed, and disappeared. He came back shortly with a glass of Campari—"compliments of the house"—before resuming his duties.

As it became dark, she was still working on her research, trying to find a reason why Klemens would make several trips, alone, to Sant'Erasmo—or to Pellestrina, Chioggia and Padua. He had frequently visited museums, especially the Museo Querini Stampalia where they had viewed the paintings by Alessandro Longhi, and a museum unfamiliar to her, the Museo d'Arte Orientale, that was located in the Ca' Pesaro palace. But he had never noted why he had visited various places more than once, even though he had meticulously recorded his thoughts about painters, people, buildings, and events—for example, about the Samurai armor in the Ca' Pesaro—everything illustrated with sketches that, together, gave a condensed picture of Venice.

She could feel that she had drunk too much, like this morning. As she was paying her bill, she was shocked at how much money she was spending. She was also surprised to see that it was already 11 o'clock.

It suddenly occurred to her to ask if there was a room available in the Hotel Cavaletto & Doge Orseolo, as she had a strong desire to move.

She quickly reached the glass studio and turned off toward the Bacino, though the gondola traffic had ceased. The illuminated windows of the hotel produced a yellow reflection in the water, like monochrome photos. She continued on, past the display window with the small glass figurines, while remembering the tiny figure representing Death. The mannequins in the clothing store still stared, smiling, out into the void, and as she came to the Calle del Salvadego and stood before the empty gondolas, in the darkness in front of the weakly-lit Hard Rock Cafe, a masculine shape got up off the ground and ran away. Instinctively, Lilli went over to the spot where, she assumed, the man had been before he fled. She thought she had gone crazy when she discovered a shoe and a leg on the sidewalk. She then recognized a body in a uniform, probably that of a policeman, and as she bent down to speak to him, she recoiled in horror, because the man at her feet was undoubtedly dead. Blood from a deep cut in his throat was flowing onto the asphalt and had already formed a large pool. The first thing she did was flee to a large crate and collapse—stunned by the alcohol and events. Just then, passers-by appeared—an old and a young couple—from the direction where the shadowy figure had disappeared. They stopped, shouted loudly, took out their smartphones, made calls and took pictures.

Only then did they notice Lilli, sitting on the plastic crate. They spoke to her, the young man wanting to know if everything was "okay," and then, if she had seen the killer.

She nodded and answered: "Only from behind."

He then asked if she had seen his face. She shook her head. "No, he immediately ran off"—she pointed a finger in the direction— "he escaped," she repeated . . . The young man (later on, she still remembered his face) had already notified the police and the water rescue, and both arrived at once. While one officer cordoned off the area and several others occupied the Hard Rock Café, one rescue team looked after Lilli, offering to let her spend the night in the hospital; in a toneless voice, she repeatedly requested to go back to her hotel. Nevertheless, she had to sit in a police boat that brought her past the moored gondolas to a police station where they took her statement.

The Commissario was Luca Zacchini by name, approximately fifty years old, with grey hair, a three-day beard, and wearing glasses with a black frame. Most noticeable was his height. He spoke fluent English, listened carefully, nodded, didn't interrupt her, and posed his next question only after long consideration.

As soon as he had taken down her personal data and asked her about her reasons for being in the city—and immediately offered his sincere condolences—he checked on his computer for the name Klemens Kuck. It surprised him that Lilli didn't believe it had been an accident, but that her husband had intentionally been pushed off the bridge.

"By whom?" the police inspector asked.

She didn't know.

The inspector was silent and checked his laptop for the file.

"This is the third murder of a policeman in the last six weeks." Zacchini said. He took off his glasses and rubbed his eyes, which made Lilli first think he was crying, but then she realized that he was tired. She felt that the incident had sobered her up. The inspector wanted to know all the details of what she had done that day, and Lilli explained that she had wanted to revisit the Hotel Cavaletto & Doge Orseolo where she and her husband had stayed three times. First of all, she was drawn to the "gondola harbor" in Bachino. She had spotted the perpetrator in poor lighting and only from behind.

The police inspector brought coffee and assured her that she would be taken back to her hotel following their conversation. He then wanted to know what her husband was doing in Venice. He was even familiar with two of his comic books that had been translated into Italian: one of his first books, "The Pig with many Faces"—it was about a detective who could assume any old face—, and "The stuttering Fortune Teller," which referred to a police woman who knew everything in advance. But he also knew the titles of several other comics, including some science-fiction stories, because his oldest son was one of Klemens' fans.

"Is it possible that he was on the trail of some mystery here in Venice?"

"He didn't talk with anyone about it, but did write down all his travels, and I've charted them on a city map of Venice."

She took the map out of her bag, unfolded it and put it on the table. The inspector pulled it over, studied it, thought a moment, had a copy made, and was then silent for a while.

"Your husband was at two locations where policemen were murdered—the first, on Pellestrina, and the second, in Giardini . . . So, it's conceivable that he was on the trail of the killer."

Lilli reached in her bag and took out a piece of paper where she had listed the routes according to the dates in the diary. Zaccini studied the times and the days when Klemens had been to the crime scenes. As it turned out, they had occurred on the days following the crimes, and during the morning hours . . .

"What do you make of that?" Zacchini wanted to know.

She confirmed that, for a time, her husband had been obsessed with crime scenes, had visited them and spoken with eyewitnesses on-site. He had also made sketches in his black notebook, and when he had used the crime and the crime scene in one of his comic books, he had meticulously adhered to his notes.

"We would like to have the black notebook with his Venetian

commentary so that we can copy it, too."

"It's all in mirror writing, and in German," Lilli replied.

"We have cryptologists and translators . . . One of my colleagues will take you by boat back to the Hotel Cavaletto, and from there accompany you to your hotel. Could you give him the notebook at that point?"

Since Lilli had made a copy anyway (which she failed to mention), she agreed.

"The file is named 'Leviathan,'" Zacchini explained. "All three killings were particularly savage. The perpetrator cut out the eyes of the first two victims and placed them beside the bodies—this time you may have startled him before he could carry out his plan." He leaned back in his chair and was silent. He then handed Lilli his business card and wrote his private phone number on it.

Lilli stood up, relieved, and again recalled that Klemens' father supposedly was or had been a police inspector in Venice.

"Do you know an inspector by the name of Galli?"

"Francesco Galli?" the Commissario asked. "Why do you ask?"

"Apparently Klemens had been looking for him in Venice and wanted to meet him."

"Why?"

"I don't know," Lilli lied. "Maybe it was about a crime that he had solved."

"The name is familiar, but I don't know him personally. As far as I know, he was let go after a stupid incident . . ."

"What incident?"

"During a hearing, he became violent with a suspect's lawyer."

"And do you have his address or telephone number?"

"I'm sorry, but you would have to contact the Registration Office and Information—I'm not authorized to provide personal information."

"And can you find out where my husband was actually staying in Venice—up to now the police don't know."

"They don't know?" the inspector asked, astonished.

"He often just vanished. He said he was inspired when no one knew where he was . . . He enjoyed disappearing . . ."

"Did you accept that? I mean, without objection?" the inspector asked.

"In the first few years that did cause conflict, but then I accepted it, if reluctantly."

"I'll let you know tomorrow . . . Did he have friends here?"

She thought of the furniture dealer Guido Alberti who had sent her Klemens' notes, but she didn't reveal that either, as her instinct dictated . . . she trusted those warnings. "No."

"Or—pardon my curiosity—a mistress? I mean, any affairs with women?"

"He wasn't a charming man," she replied, though it wasn't true.

The inspector typed on the keyboard of his laptop and didn't speak.

"As I told you, Inspector Galli is no longer in service. He is registered in Padua where he has rented an apartment near the Piazza Eremitani . . . to be precise, number 10 on the Via Risorgimento."

Lilli reached for the ballpoint pen and noted the address on the map of Venice that she had gotten back.

Of course, she knew that the Piazza Eremitani was the location of the Scrovegni Chapel with the frescoes by Giotto that she had twice—once as a student and once with Klemens—visited and admired.

"Do you want to contact him?"

". . . I think I'd better go back to my hotel now."

The inspector stood up and seemed to be deep in thought. He abruptly said his goodbyes, then left the room and closed the door behind him.

A few moments later a policewoman appeared who, full of sympathy, accompanied her to the boat and rode with her to the scene of the crime where the victim still lay—covered by a grey plastic tarp—and police and forensics officers went about their work in disposable white overalls with hoods and wearing high white shoe covers. In front of the Hard Rock Café, uniformed police were still taking personal information and statements from guests, small little flags on the asphalt marked tracks and evidence. From the hotel windows, nearly all lit, guests followed the events on the Bacino. Lilli hurried on. She didn't want to spend any more time here.

In the lobby of the Hotel Diana, she asked her companion to wait, then handed over the notes in mirror writing for which she received a receipt. It was just after midnight when she fell asleep, exhausted, and sometime after eight o'clock when she woke up.

5

The Furniture Store, Signor Alberti, Nicole and Struppi

From the moment she opened her eyes, she had thought about the murdered policeman and the stranger who had fled.

Before she rushed off to speak with Roberto in Caffè Florian, she took the little mosaic stone from the Basilica in her fingers, to make contact with Klemens, but everything she did, now seemed trivial.

Her gaze came to rest on her empty suitcase, and instantly on the second case that had erroneously been delivered to her new room. But she didn't get upset that the houseboy had made the same mistake twice.

Before she could form another thought, there was a knock at the door.

"I'm the idiot who follows you around with his suitcase," the man said, standing there, assessing her through the half-open door.

"Haven't we met before?" he asked. "Possibly at 'Am Heumarkt' in Vienna?"

"Yes," Lilli said, hesitantly.

"Did you live there before the gas explosion?"

"We had just left on a trip . . . But I do know that the writer lost his life in his apartment."

"Then you are Frau Dr. Kuck and work in the Kunsthistorisches Museum, and I am Michael Aldrian . . ."

". . . You've since moved away?"

"Yes."

"Weren't you prompter at the Vienna State Opera?"

"Exactly, *Maestro Suggeritore*, but I had a hearing loss and had to give up my profession . . . I'm now living my second life, so to speak." He smiled.

"I opened your suitcase by mistake, and since I had a headache. I borrowed some tablets," Lilli said.

"Is the skull still there?" Aldrian asked, without further explanation. "I need it for my shows," he added.

Lilli still hadn't opened the door all the way, and nodded "Didn't you miss your suitcase?"

"No. I myself conjured it into your room, because I suddenly had to go to Sant'Erasmo," he laughed.

"Sant'Erasmo?"

"I live on Sant'Erasmo and help a friend who is Maestro Suggeritore in Venice . . . in the Teatro la Fenice . . . with the production of *Don Giovanni* . . . I have all of Mozart's operas in my head. At other times, my colleague fills in as conductor for operas by Verdi, Bellini or Rossini and Donizetti . . ."

"As conductor?"

"I told you he is Maestro Suggeritore . . . That means not just a prompter, but also a conductor . . . By the way, I had conversations with your husband every once in a while . . . Is he also in Venice?"

"No."

"What is he working on right now?"

"He's dead."

Aldrian was stunned and didn't speak.

"He had an accident . . ." she went on, "here in Venice."

"I am very sorry."

Lilli nodded.

"May I come in for just a moment—I'm beginning to feel like I'm in a confessional."

She could only stammer "Oh, I completely forgot," and opened the door. "The suitcase is here by the chair," she added.

"Thank you!"

As he entered the room and bent down for his luggage, Lilli sighed.

He opened the suitcase, felt the bottom beneath the objects and clothing, and suddenly pulled out the skull.

Lilli took a step back.

"It's not real . . . Magic is the pinnacle of mimicry and imitation . . . Even the tricks we present are imitations of happenstance . . ." He took the false teeth out of the suitcase, with one hand pretended that they were speaking, and, as ventriloquist, introduced Pagliacci. "The teeth have all been extracted, I'll move on into the mouth itself . . ." It actually seemed to Lilli that Aldrian hadn't moved his lips. A moment later, he put the false teeth and the skull back in the suitcase.

"I apologize for my indiscretion. I need to rearrange some things in my program."

He offered her his hand, nodded, and hurried out into the hallway.

As Lilli closed the door, she felt like laughing, but couldn't quite do it. Just then, there was another knock on the door, and when she opened it, the magician was standing there again, a ticket in his hand.

"I forgot to give you a ticket for the show, tomorrow evening at 6 p.m. in the Hotel Excelsior . . . Can I make up for that lapse?"

She was delighted, took the ticket, and promised to come.

The magician's visit, as strange as it was, had been a relief, even if it hadn't been able to ward off the images of the previous night. She took her iPad out of her suitcase, connected with the hotels Wi-Fi network, and attempted to find out, in both English and German, more details about the policeman's murder that continued to haunt her. It was tedious work, but she finally found the latest information in a German tabloid. The article also mentioned the two previous police killings. The murder on Pellestrina had taken place early in the morning, right at the entrance to the cemetery at the vaporetto station, the crime in the Giardini, however, happened at noon. Then they described the nighttime attack at the Bacino. The throats of all three victims had been cut, and two of them had had their eyes gouged out. Lilli already knew that. She was also familiar with the piazza at the cemetery on Pellestrina. She suddenly remembered that Klemens' suitcase had never arrived in Vienna. In the difficult days following Klemens' return, she had reported it missing, but hadn't really worried about it. Had Aldrian's magic suitcase in the hotel reminded her of that fact? So, it was all about the suitcase, and she was secretly upset that for so long she had paid no attention to the reference or hadn't even understood it as such.

She showered, and now she thought again of the name Guido Alberti, the furniture dealer, who had supposedly been friends with Klemens . . . After she had put on makeup, she checked on her iPad . . . As a matter of fact, after she entered the name Guido Alberti, she did locate the office of the furniture store, *Mobili Italiani*, on the Calle del Frutarol. She automatically took out the city map with Klemens' routes and looked for the street. He had never mentioned it in his notes. Why not? Had he really had a mistress? And had he lived with her? She became restless, and without having eaten breakfast, went down into the street and hurried to Caffè Florian to speak with Roberto . . . "Thoughts are like the union of two DNAs: you never know what the result will be," Klemens had joked before he had created his last comic book, *Casanova*. It was full of obscene pictures because, in his works, our sex life should have as much importance as all other human traits. For that book he had made several long trips to Venice. Could he possibly have met other women? It didn't matter that he was dead—she was jealous, even posthumously—she was probably even more insulted to be deceived in retrospect, because she no longer had the chance to confront him. Just the thought of her vulnerability, her helplessness was painful. Then, suddenly and without provocation, she saw the dead policeman, but she didn't want to think about him. She didn't want to learn any details of his private life: whether he had children, a wife . . . It was fear of further injury that made her think like that. Moreover, her mental state was changing. Her condition changed several times a day, the only thing that remained the same was her "camouflage," as she called it, because her self-control was still intact . . .

She fled with the map back in the direction of her hotel, and from there, further up the street. She noticed yet another display window with glass animal jewelry: marvelously delicate insects—stag beetles, crickets, grasshoppers, rhinoceros beetles—and two salamanders with their black-and-yellow exterior that made her think of the reflection of the illuminated hotel windows in the nighttime water of the Bacino . . . And, simultaneously, of the murdered man and, again, of Klemens . . . It was obvious that she needed a break. She wanted nothing more than to lie on the beach and let her thoughts roam, or to stroll along the seashore . . . Her gaze was still focused on the colorful glass butterflies, on a scorpion and a dragonfly . . . After all, she did have that little gold mosaic stone in her sunglasses case . . . Even the extra-large wasps on the bottom shelf with their black-and-yellow bodies made her think of the murder.

A bit later she came to even narrower alleys and, by chance, passed the Cioccolateria VizioVirtù on the Calle del Forner, that she knew from visits together with Klemens who had always killed time there. She entered and had a breakfast of cake and hot chocolate . . . It was clear to her that she was in an unstable condition—on the one hand, she wanted seclusion; on the other, she was afraid of it. She also didn't know whether she wanted to forget Klemens or always have him on her mind. She had become a child, a traumatized little girl, she thought, as she ate the cake. They all say that, after a death, you should take time to get back to normal life. If time passed more slowly, in slow-motion so to speak, then did that open doors to new impressions, new experiences, new encounters?

That made her think of the dreams of "Little Nemo." Even as an adult, Klemens had loved the comic book series "Little Nemo in Slumberland" by Winsor McCay. The book was filled with fantastic

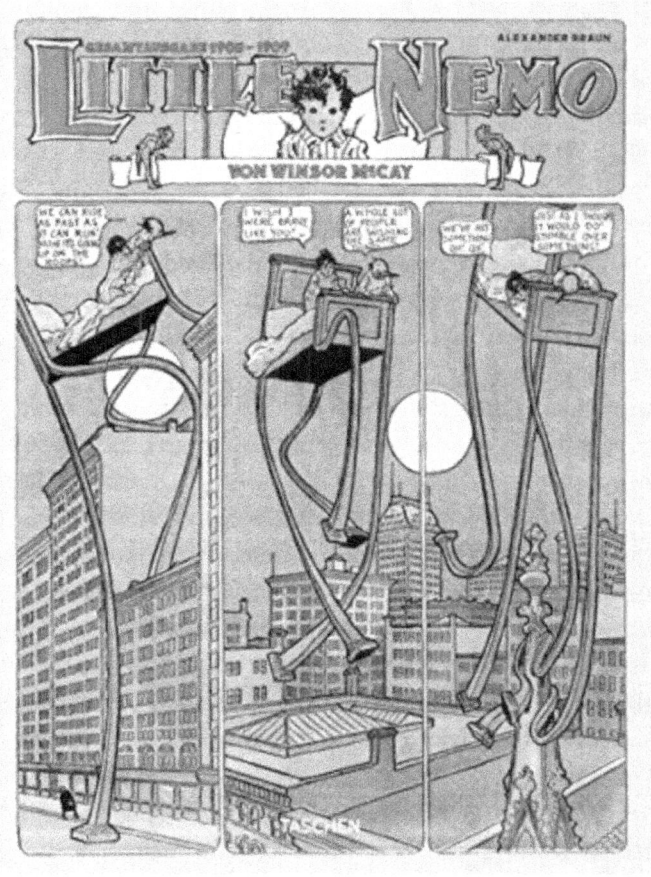

dream scenes that always developed into dangerous situations and only had a happy ending when he woke up in his own bed. Surrealistic pictures dominated the scenes. Klemens especially liked the figure of the king of "Slumberland," Morpheus, and Nemo's adversary, Flip, who later becomes his companion and wears a hat with the motto "Wake up." For Lilli, Nemo was the perfect example of the loneliness of children whose real life frequently took place in daydreams. That had always attracted her, but also upset her—yet another example of how most of her feelings and thoughts were full of contradictions. One day (she had just turned fourteen), she suddenly understood that everyone's thoughts and behavior were contradictory. Logic, she later realized, was a separate language, so to speak, that mathematical stenography people used to translate the inexplicable into comprehensible units. As she grew older, the more eager she became to discover contradictions in everyone and everything. In her eyes, everyone was disjoined, some more, others less, and most people had many worlds in their head that existed while contradicting each other.

She bought a lot of candy and went on looking for Alberti's furniture store, which she discovered just around the next corner. The three or four display windows had mattresses, upholstered furniture covered by sheets, along with small tables. The office was kitty-corner across the street, identifiable by the sign "Italian Furniture—Wholesale." Lilli didn't hesitate, and entered the building. Since the streets were so narrow, the office space was quite dark. A young secretary was just drawing something with magic markers, and a middle-aged gentleman in suit and tie was leafing through a large-format furniture catalog. She introduced herself, and he immediately stood up and came over. At that moment, a wire-haired fox terrier leaped out from under a desk and began to bark.

The furniture dealer spoke perfect English: "I am Guido Alberti . . . A friend of your husband . . . I was certain that you would come," he said, with a serious expression. He offered her a chair. "That is my daughter"—he pointed to the young girl that Lilli had first thought was a secretary—"Nicole . . . I sent you Klemens' diary, we worked closely together."

Lilli now realized that Nicole had Down syndrome. Lilli unintentionally had a questioning look, and Guido Alberti reacted to it.

"For a long time, I worked for the police as a forensics expert. I now work as a private detective. Officially, I am the CEO of our furniture business that belongs to my wife, because I carry out investigations where it is better to remain incognito. I met Klemens in Caffè Florian a year-and-a-half ago. We had long conversations about crime in Venice. I showed him scenes of crimes and, when possible, actual police files. At the end he was on the trail of a man suspected of killing three policemen . . . Klemens was obsessed with the case, because after the comic book about Casanova and his breakout from the lead chambers, he needed to write a crime-novel comic book that again is set in Venice."

Lilli nodded. "Wasn't he working on a Samurai story? In any event, he told me he was," she changed topics, just to see what Alberti would say.

"That's possible, we didn't see each other every day. But he frequently visited the Museo d'Arte Orientale in the Ca' Pesaro, that I know for sure, and he sometimes told me things about Japanese fighting techniques . . ."

Lilli thought for a moment. "Was he looking for someone?" she wanted to know.

"For whom? I mean, aside from the cop killer?"

"Did he ever mention a Police Inspector Francesco Galli?"

"Galli? No. What made you think of Galli?"

"He knew him . . . Maybe he sought his advice, as he did with you?" Lilli kept fibbing.

"Galli . . . I seem to recall the name."

"In what context?"

In the meantime, Alberti's daughter had stood up, bent down, picked up the dog, and set it on her lap.

Lilli told herself that she would now have to try and get more out of Alberti.

"Why didn't you write your address on the envelope you sent with Klemens' Venice notebook," she asked.

"You must have forgotten to write our return address," Alberti said to his daughter in Italian, annoyed.

Nicole shook her head. It looked as if she were about to cry.

"It's okay," Alberti said in a comforting tone, and stroked her hand, but tears were already streaming down her cheeks, and the dog started barking.

"The dog belonged to Klemens," the former forensic expert said. "One day he just turned up with it, insisting it was a stray mutt that had been following him around."

Since Nicole studied him warily, he translated his information into Italian. Nicole instantly stopped sobbing and insisted that Struppi belonged to her.

"Where are you going to keep him?" Alberti asked her, irritated.

Nicole was close to tears again.

"He belongs to you, if Signor Alberti allows you to keep him," Lilli interjected in English.

Alberti inhaled demonstratively, grimaced to indicate that he was gradually losing his mind, and nodded.

"*Bene,*" he briefly uttered, though it wasn't clear what he meant by it.

"Well, fine," Nicole added, petulantly.

"How could Klemens take a dog into his hotel room?" Lilli asked, changing topics.

"Klemens lived at our house. In a telephone conversation, I promised he could hide out at our place if he felt he was being followed. So, he showed up with his suitcase and didn't even look for a hotel."

"He was here right from the start?"

"Yes. Didn't you know that?" Guido Alberti asked. "If you want, I can show you his living quarters. They are modest, of course, but he liked them."

The three of them, along with the dog, went to the business across the street. Alberti took out his keys and unlocked the door. They first went through the warehouse with the large display windows. Lilli had the impression that she was being projected onto a movie screen and from that vantage point could see the empty theater auditorium that was the narrow street outside. From time to time a figure rushed past, but no one actually stopped to study the furniture. At the same time, Lilli had to think of Klemens' grave where he would eventually turn to dust.

At the end of the second showcase, a wooden wall set a type of living niche apart from the rest of the room. Nicole proudly opened the door. Lilli gazed into a very small room with a freshly-made double bed, a standing lamp, a desk and chair, and when she opened a side door, she could see an even narrower wardroom space with Klemens' clothing lying on shelves, his suitcase on the floor, presumably empty, Lilli thought. The third door revealed a bath with toilet, along with a window that provided muted daylight.

Guido Alberti was mentioning that he offered everything to Klemens at no charge, and Nicole invited Lilli to live here as well.

Back in the office, Alberti assured her that she could pick up Klemens' clothing and suitcase at any time. Furthermore, he requested the phone number of her hotel and her e-mail address, as he handed her his business card.

Lilli was stunned as she made her way to the Rialto Bridge and boarded the vaporetto to visit the Giardini. On the way she called Guido Alberti and asked him where, exactly, the policeman had been killed in the Giardini Publici . . . Alberti described a place on the bank of the Canal di San Marco . . . There was an asphalt path that led to a stone stairway. The killer must have been lurking there, waiting for his victim, and then made his escape by motorboat after slitting the policeman's throat.

Lilli didn't get off the waterbus until they reached Sant'Elena, and set off on foot in the shade of vinegar trees. She didn't head straight for the scene of the crime, but sat down on a bench in a more bustling spot, closed her eyes, opened them, and noticed a blooming cherry laurel bush that smelled intoxicating. A dark cloud passed, a few drops of rain fell, but then quit. When she naturally thought of Klemens, she forced herself to think of something else . . . That was hard, because, after all, she had come to see the spot where one of the murders had taken place . . . She had always been for humane treatment of criminals and against the death penalty—but now she felt hate. At the same time, she was afraid of the perpetrator. Why had Klemens always been interested in cruelty and violence? He had always responded to her questions with the same stock answers. He wanted to examine the essence of people who kill, who wage war, and who view military events as "history." Most of the significant personalities in history were murderers, he repeatedly insisted, he compared them with Mafia bosses who are involved in gang wars. Lilli eventually quit asking.

Meanwhile she had taken the candy out of her purse and begun to stuff the chocolate-covered ginger-, fig-, and apricot slices into her mouth. A baby blackbird scurried back and forth at her feet. The pigeons, she decided, moved about more leisurely. On a bench in the shade, directly across from Lilli, a woman was sleeping with a green-yellow patterned baseball cap down over her face, a duffel bag in her lap. Her husband's head was resting on a backpack, and he, too, was asleep. His red sports cap had also slipped down over his eyes so that only part of his purple-mirrored sunglasses was visible, while his strikingly large feet were in sneakers with air-cushioned soles and pointed upward like shark's fins. A chrome watch with a black face gleamed at his wrist. Just then she realized that birds in the trees and shrubs had been chirping the entire time. She liked the sounds, and they comforted her. The woman opposite her was wearing jeans and a gold-colored wristwatch with a white face. Lilli noticed that she had lovely fingers and was wearing a wedding ring, as was her husband. The two of them were probably in their seventies. Lilli had noticed all that while putting a chocolate bonbon in her mouth. She knew she would rapidly put-on weight if she kept this up, but at the same time she insisted it wouldn't happen. And she suddenly realized that she also wouldn't visit the crime scene. What was the point?

She left the park, strolled under the branches of the vinegar trees, back to the Sant'Elena vaporetto station, and was relieved. Why should she let herself be roped into Klemens' curiosity? In any case, she now had a lead, and that was Guido Alberti. Of course, she had no idea how things would progress, but she could wait—if not for an eternity. A flock of pigeons and a sparrow came over and let an elderly woman and her grandchild, a girl, feed them white bread.

In the vaporetto it suddenly occurred to her that everything she had learned about Klemens fit together. That he had gone underground, that no one would think to look for him in a furniture store, that a young girl with Down syndrome was involved, and that he had not only picked up the white wire-haired fox terrier but also named it "Struppi." Time after time he had been on the lookout for hiding places where he could work undisturbed. One time it had been a neighbor's apartment, another time an empty building where she had driven out to meet him, then a closed lighthouse, and, finally, a sailboat on Lake Neusiedl that he had rented—without mentioning it to her at all. He had always been attracted to people with Down syndrome because of their foreign world, their "other way of thinking," as he called it. Through conversations with them, he attempted to better understand his own subconscious, and he also enjoyed giving each one of them a little something. In general, he loved plants and animals, Lilli recalled, collected books that illustrated them, and had always wanted to have a dog, though he never got one, as he was afraid he would lose his freedom. In Hergé's comic books, "Struppi" was, of course, a fox terrier, and that's why it was natural for Klemens to choose this name for the dog. He never would have called it a "stray mutt." He loved "Tim and Struppi" in *The Adventures of Tintin*. Since childhood he had owned all the books and could retell them down to the smallest detail. Before he began his studies at the Academy of Fine Arts Vienna (which he didn't complete), he had even composed a volume in Hergé's style, but hadn't given it a title. Still, "Struppi" had haunted Klemens up to his death . . .

Back in her hotel room, she finally found two messages from the porter who—as always—was always off duty by the afternoon. Since she felt tired, she lay down on the bed and read the messages bearing the stamp of the hotel: at 1:26 p.m. Guido Alberti reported that "ex-Inspector" Galli (as he called him) was now staying on the island of Pellestrina—he had even found out the address. Alberti also offered to pick her up tomorrow at 10 a.m. and escort her.

The second message, at 1:31 p.m., came from a South Tirolean who claimed he was working on a translation of William Shakespeare's complete works, and informed her that a Signor Egon Blanc, who had been a patron and admirer of Klemens Kuck, sent an invitation. Then there was a telephone number. How did this translator (whose name on the message she couldn't make out and therefore must be some kind of abbreviation) . . . how did he know that she was in Venice and was staying at the Hotel Diana? And who was he, after all? And how had he come up with her name? No doubt he must have known Klemens, as must the unknown host named Blanc. She put the two messages on the nightstand, slept for a few hours, went into the bathroom, showered, and took a sleeping tablet. She thought about Klemens' suitcase the whole time . . . She at least wanted to find out if there was anything in it worth saving. Strange, what part suitcases were playing in her life . . . She took the little gold mosaic stone out of her sunglasses case and placed it on the glass top of her nightstand.

6
Chioggia

When she woke up the next morning and gazed out the window, she could see a delicate rainbow above the roof of the taller opposite building. She stood at the window as it began to rain.

She appeared at breakfast punctually, but realized that she had forgotten the little mosaic stone in her room. She immediately retraced her steps, carefully wrapped the little stone in tissue paper, and put it in her pants pocket . . . took both messages with her and—back in the lobby—asked the porter about the name of yesterday's second caller that she hadn't been able to read on the note.

"Signor Lanz," the porter explained, after glancing at the piece of paper.

That didn't mean anything to her. She packed the two notes in her purse, paused, and glanced at her watch. It was already 10:20, she was late. But Guido Alberti wasn't on time either, as it turned out—he and Nicole were just coming around the corner with Struppi, and he laughed when he spotted her. The dog barked, and Nicole waved to her. Lilli was surprised, because at that moment she hadn't expected to see the two of them.

"I found Galli by accident!" Guido Alberti began. "For as long as he was on the police force, we were almost colleagues." The private detective and furniture dealer was wearing a nifty summer outfit. His pants featured an asymmetrical leaf pattern that reminded Lilli of uncontrolled growth in a garden. His shirt, on the other hand, was embellished with a colorful Christian heart design: burning, crowned with thorns, or pierced by lances.

"Francesco Galli had an unblemished record, but in one isolated instance he lost control during an interrogation and had thrown a paperweight and several boxed files at a suspect's woman lawyer. Francesco's statement about the incident was more than strange: he blamed an old billionaire who spent enormous sums on refugees, invalids, orphans, and other worthwhile causes, to have purposely misled him about one of the man's protégés."

Just then Lilli felt Nicole unaffectedly take her hand as she spoke with Struppi. Alberti translated her commands: "Don't bite . . . Only when I say 'bite'! Otherwise, that's a no-no!"

They had to wait at the Lido Santa Maria station because the bus for the Pellestrina cemetery (where the first policeman had been killed) only left every hour on the hour. Lilli preferred to wait in the building beside the dock and from that vantage point gaze out the window at the light show of sun and water on the hull of a small vaporetto. She had never noticed that before: the flashing and fluttering, the disappearance and reappearance, and the blinding brightness. It allowed her to imagine a world of light and darkness. Lilli saw herself reflected in one of the glass panes and had to look through herself. In the distance she could just make out the Campanile and the Doge's Palace and this or that vaporetto on the water. Maybe the hulls of ships with the flickering black and bright-white blotches was something like a separate continent that was illuminated by lightning, she asked herself.

She interrupted her train of thought and hurried over to the Line #11 bus where Nicole and Guido had already found seats, with Struppi sound asleep at their feet. Nicole had saved a seat for Lilli by simply stretching out lengthwise across two plastic seats. She happily withdrew her legs so that Lilli had a seat, the white wire-hair fox terrier blinked one eye, and Guido said in English: "My daughter saved that seat for you!" At that moment, Lilli noticed that Nicole was wearing black, like she herself: black pants, a black T-shirt, and a light-weight black jacket. Her fingernails were brightly painted and her sunglasses had a chic red frame.

The bus drove off with a sudden lurch that almost threw Lilli out of her seat. Alberti laughed, but recomposed himself and helped her back into her seat. In his suit, he looked like a crazed priest, she thought. The Christian hearts made him seem somehow unreal. Lilli sat facing the rear of the bus which, she felt, was unpleasant, and clung to a vertical aluminum pole with one hand so that—if the driver braked suddenly—she wouldn't be ejected from her seat.

It occurred to her that never before in her life had she understood herself less than now. But that was the reason, she assumed, why she was now rushing into adventures. At the moment she didn't want to return home, she thought, the past should become a memory, something that gradually resembled a dream.

A man, facing her from across the aisle, was playing cards on his iPad, his wife read the newspaper *La Repubblica*, with two suitcases standing vertically behind them.

"Not more suitcases!" Lilli thought, and saw that Nicole, sitting upright, was staring at the luggage, her mouth open wide. The girl noticed that Lilli was watching her, stuck out her arm and pointed at the tottering suitcases. Although the bus roared on, the two passengers continued their activities. In the meantime, even Guido Alberti had turned to the suitcases and silently laughed as he turned back around. Suddenly, when the bus suddenly braked, the stored luggage fell over and crashed to the floor with a crunching and rattling noise. The woman with the newspaper raised her eyebrows and glanced sternly at her companion. She put away the printed pages with an angry gesture, and the man leaped up. The iPad was now on his seat, as he tried to set the suitcases down horizontally in the jolting bus, so that he could check to see if anything in them had been damaged. Lilli could see that they were flowerpots, and from the man's expression she could tell that several must have been broken. The woman smiled, gloating, but you couldn't miss the fact that she was still angry. Just then Nicole began to cry and Struppi to bark, until Guido Alberti took her in his arms and calmed her down. Struppi instantly stopped barking. Alberti reached in his pocket and tossed the terrier a treat which the dog gulped down. Nicole was afraid, Alberti explained, that the broken flower pots would bring bad luck, you can't talk her out of it . . . Many times she's even right.

The bus arrived at the Alberoni ferry and jolted its way on board. Lilli remembered the lighthouses on the seashore from an earlier trip with Klemens. Nicole still was pressing her face against her father's chest and her sobbing gradually subsided until she fell back onto her seat. But she still avoided even a glance at the suitcases or their owners. Lilli preferred to remain silent, since she didn't know what effect her words would have on Nicole . . . The ferry slowly began to move and steered sluggishly out to sea.

It wasn't until they landed on Pellestrina that the girl had calmed down. The bus began to race off again, and on her left, she could see the endlessly long *murazzi*, walls that protect the island from seawater flooding. Where they were lower, now and then a treetop, an empty beach, or sight of the open sea flashed past. The view of the right side of the lagoon was, at first, concealed by thick reeds or shrubs.

Time after time the bus halted at bus stops, where Lilli could catch a glimpse of small factories, dockyards, fenced-in areas, and row houses with clothes drying on the balconies. She then saw wooden huts in the water, covered with tarpaulins, for the tools of the fishermen. They seemed to her to be junkyards in the lagoon. Meadows alternated with construction cranes, factory buildings, church towers, and modest front yards. In one of the parks, surrounded by a yellow wall, children were playing badminton. Other lagoon inlets flitted past the bus window, a soccer field, a traffic sign, or a vast parking lot with a single car. Lilli noticed that there was a great deal of traffic on this narrow road. A line of cars had already jammed up behind the bus since vehicles could only pass at bus stops. The bus itself was behind a truck that was carrying a gigantic construction machine. There were few people out and about: a couple of young bald men, some girls, all stylishly dressed.

The mesmerizing images were also hard for Lilli to absorb. The sun was, by now, blinding and scorching. Now and then, a white or blue fishing boat in the void.

They finally arrived at the end of the line where, in place of the murrazzi, they could see the high yellow walls of the cemetery. Everyone got off the bus, some passengers were in a hurry to get home, others trotted down to the waiting platform where the vaporetto to Chioggia would dock. But Guido Alberti set off to the cemetery, past newly-planted trees, and encouraged Nicole to follow him. Meanwhile, Struppi was pulling Nicole along on the leash. The three stopped in the shade of the entrance, while Lilli waited by the bus, because under no circumstances did she want to see any more graves.

"What about Commissario Galli?" she called out.

"Later. He isn't home now."

"Where is he?"

"At the moment, no one knows. I phoned before we left . . . While we're waiting, we'll view the cemetery, and by then he'll probably be home."

Since Alberti and Nicole were enthusiastically waving to her and Struppi had begun barking, she hesitantly approached them and learned that Alberti wanted to show her the spot where one of the three policemen was killed. She stopped and nodded.

He went on to say that his mother was also buried here. Alberti then hurried off with Nicole and Struppi, but Lilli turned back and resolutely went to the waiting platform for the vaporetto to Chioggia.

"What an idiot!" she thought, furious.

Alberti should have realized that, after her husband's funeral, she wouldn't want to see another cemetery. First, she was determined to not look back, but then she did anyway. Since the path to the vaporetto station was downhill, she got a glimpse of the cemetery's vacant entrance gate on the hill, and instantly fled to the waiting platform where the waterbus was just docking. An unimaginably large crowd streamed off, with their packages and boxes, among them an old woman in a wheelchair and a Vespa motor scooter. There were also tourists with bicycles, helmets, and racing gloves who spoke German. Lilli didn't dare look up and see Alberti, Nicole, and Struppi; just the opposite, she was relieved when the vaporetto finally pulled away.

When she looked out at the open sea, she could see huge construction cranes on the horizon. They were needed for the construction of the floodgates that were built around Venice many years ago to keep *acqua alta* from the city.

On the shore of a small island ahead, workers were climbing all over an enormous mountain of gravel. From a distance, it looked like some sea monster, lying dead on the rocky sand, while being carved up by tiny human beings. "Leviathan," she thought, and the three files on the three police killings came to mind that Inspector Luca Zacchini—she remembered his name—had shown her.

She toyed with the thought of stopping on her way back and looking for Klemens' father, the deposed Police Inspector Francesco Galli, simply because she was curious about how he looked . . . Maybe he would be more approachable than Klemens' mother in Hallstatt. Presumably he knew nothing about his son's death, and Lilli felt she owed it to Klemens to notify his father.

Time and time again long jetties poked out into the water. A white devastated shipwreck was secured to one of them.

In front of her stood an old man with sunglasses on a lanyard around his neck. He wore a sun hat that was too small, and his mouth was open. Now she also discovered the woman who was waiting on one of the wooden benches, also wearing sunglasses. It wasn't until Lilli noticed the seeing-eye dog on the floor that she realized the couple couldn't see. It occurred to her that, above all else, she recognized human tragedies, as if she were searching for them, and she also realized that she was not alone with her life's pain . . . It was arrogant to only think of herself and her own sorrows. The bind man, for example, lived in his own world, he traveled with public transportation and had practice doing so. In the meantime, he had sat down beside his wife. They exchanged a few words, and their seeing-eye dog listened attentively, like a model student. It was impossible for Lilli to imagine how two blind people could get around without images in their heads, read books in braille, or go on trips to explore other cities and countries . . . It must be strangely beautiful—her thoughts strayed—to have your own world, not as a person, but like a bird in the sky that could look down on the earth, or like a fish in water that glowed in the deep sea. She thought of the little mosaic stone, and felt she had found the key to Klemens' death through her investigations: piece by piece, the smallest insights would join together and ultimately form a mosaic.

The vaporetto reached the Chioggia harbor with its hundreds of blue and white sailboats, their masts jutting into the sky. Her thoughts were like a Moebius strip, she realized, they always came back to Klemens. Incidentally, he had been a great admirer of "Moebius," the cartoonist Jean Giraud, whom he had visited in Paris before the great man's death. Giraud, as "Moebius," had created unique fantasy worlds, but he was also friends with a cult leader who insisted he was in contact with aliens. The extraterrestrials supposedly wanted to save mankind from the apocalypse and take them up into outer space. In the 1980s, Giraud and his family had lived in Tahiti for two years as a member of the cult. His work was voluminous and wide-ranging. Both Klemens and Lilli admired *The Star Wanderers* and especially *The Incal*—two multiple-volume comic book series. In *The Star Wanderers*, the main characters Stell and Atan discovered a galaxy and thus a completely new reality.

Illustrations from the comics now mingled with the sight of ships in the harbor and the reflections on the water beneath the huge sky.

She was familiar with Chioggia's Corso del Popolo, the long straight road from the harbor, with its numerous cafés, small shops, and bars. She had been to the small town twice with her husband, and they had stayed in the Hotel Grande Italia, directly at the harbor.

Still underway, she was uncertain whether she'd be able to enter the hotel or not. But now that she was back on land, she walked

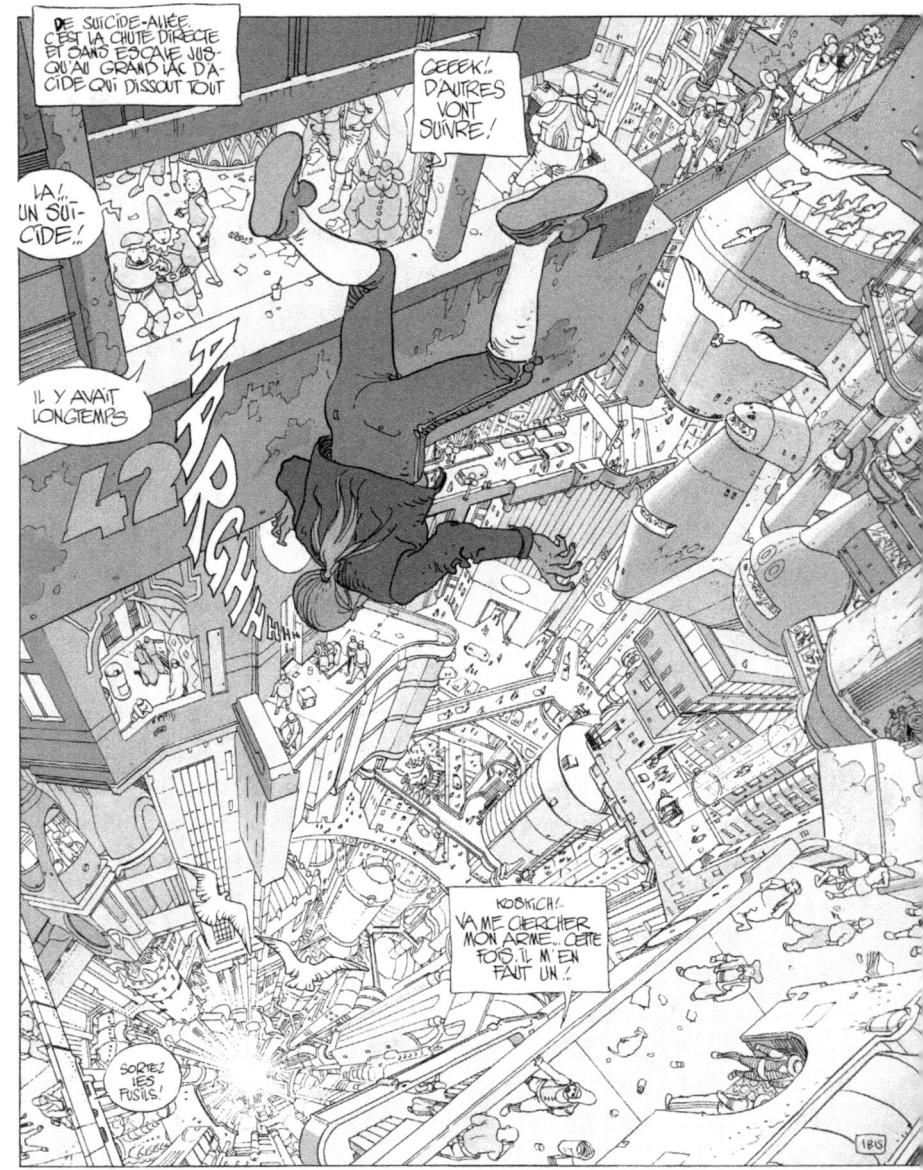

right in, and found at the reception area (that was unstaffed) several folded city maps. She took one—since she remembered from her previous stay that Chioggia was depicted on the front and Venice on the back—when a young attractive woman rushed over and asked how she could be of assistance. Since Lilli didn't really know why she had come in to the hotel, she pretended to want to know if the hotel was open in winter.

"Yes, the entire year!" answered the receptionist, and handed Lilli a business card.

She then wandered up the street, bought a new glasses case at an optician's store and tucked the little mosaic stone inside, threw the paper bag away, and found a seat at an outdoor café. From the sidewalk, so to speak, she watched the people as they passed by, just as she had done as a child in Hamburg.

In Chioggia, she always had the impression she was at one of those original locations from Fellini's movie *Amarcord*. She opened the city map, looked for the café where she presently sat, and pondered if she should take a harbor tour, when the smartphone in her purse rang. She must have accidentally activated it.

"Where are you?" Alberti asked, without so much as a greeting. He promised to be on the next vaporetto. Nicole has been pestering him to take her to Chioggia. So Alberti suggested that they meet in the Osteria Penzo that Lilli knew quite well.

An old man in a beige suit with a matching hat slowly rode by on his bicycle. Bulging transparent shopping bags hung from the handlebars. He had two miniature flags in the Italian national colors flying from the rear cargo rack.

Why, she asked herself, why had Klemens come to Chioggia twice? Was it for pleasure, or did he have a reason to be there? . . . Or was he with a woman after all?

The old man almost fell as he turned off into a side street. High up in the sky, Lilli saw a flock of seagulls where one lone gull broke away and sailed off in the sunlight—bright, white, parts of its wings almost transparent, it seemed to her. "Vespa" motor scooters and "Ape" three-wheeled transporters—"wasps" and "bees" according to the Italians—drove past, and bicycles with and without electric motors, children riding in the front or rear cargo racks, or dogs at the feet of Vespa drivers, in baskets on the handlebars or over the back wheel. One thing she had noticed on previous trips were the many disabled people who lived in the city. Lilli assumed that the locals didn't put them in nursing homes, but took care of their relatives themselves. She kept an eye out for the disabled, not out of any malicious intentions, but rather out of curiosity. She didn't have to wait long, as a fifty- to sixty-year-old man appeared under the awning, supported by two crutches. The fingers on both of his hands were adorned with old gold signet rings—Lilli counted seven in all—and two wedding rings. Apparently, he was a widower, or else he had inherited them from his parents . . . The disabled man sat down at the small bar—three feet from her—ordered coffee, said hello to everyone, told jokes, flirted with the young waitress, and coughed. His false teeth obviously didn't fit properly. A keychain swung from his waistband with several keys, one was very large. Lilli saw two old women in black sitting in front of her, wearing cardigans sweaters in spite of the heat. Both had glasses, short grey hair, and the more corpulent one had large gold earrings.

It now seemed silly to assume that Klemens had met a lover here . . . He must have been following up on some tip, she presumed, or following a trail. She paid her bill and got up.

Soon after that, she arrived at the Osteria Penzo where she and Klemens had had dinner, sat down at a table in front of the restaurant on one side of the narrow street. She was briefly startled when a motorcycle drove past and just barely missed her, she then glanced into the restaurant and saw it was packed, ordered a glass of wine, and went back to her table outside.

After a while, Nicole and her father appeared. Nicole was perspiring and breathing heavily, Alberti, however, was pensive, practically introverted. Lilli suspected that the two of them had argued on the way. The greying host and, later, the two waitresses were exceptionally polite while taking their orders. Nicole wanted a platter of fried fish for all of them, followed by tiramisu. When she then went to the restroom, Albert confided in Lilli: he had located the second home of his former colleague Galli close to the bus station by the cemetery in Pellestrina. But Galli wasn't home. So, while Nicole was waiting at the vaporetto stations, he questioned several neighbors about the man and, finally, a retired woman informed him that Galli was presently staying with his girlfriend in Chioggia—in fact, in the Calle Larga Bersaglio, diagonally across from the Osteria Penzo. Alberti pointed to a house with balconies. Lilli now understood why Klemens had been on Pellestrina and in Chioggia. He had visited his father or at least intended to meet with him.

"Why are you looking for Signor Galli?" she asked.

"You're asking me? You were the one who brought him to my attention . . . and I think he has a few things to tell us . . . In any event, you can do me a big favor," he hesitated and, when Lilli didn't respond, went on: "Nicole received an invitation for a magic event at 6 p.m. this evening in the Hotel Excelsior. The show is especially for children with Down syndrome. My wife doesn't get home until later tonight and felt that Nicole and I should go on ahead. Of course, I'd rather stay here in the osteria to see how things develop." Eventually he would check out the apartment of the woman where Galli might be staying, he added.

Lilli nodded, and he took out his briefcase and handed her two tickets.

"My daughter would never forgive me if she missed the show."

Lilli didn't mention to Alberti that she already had an invitation, since she didn't want to explain the incident with the suitcase. Aldrian hadn't mentioned that it was a private function, and she was suddenly looking forward to it.

"The entire affair is an initiative of the Egon Blanc Foundation— do you know him? He is a billionaire but, other than his closest associates, no one has ever seen him up close. Some insist he's over a hundred years old."

Lilli's thoughts were already elsewhere.

"I want to know what Galli looks like," she said.

Alberti gave her a questioning look, hesitated, then took his smartphone out of his jacket pocket, typed on the display, and put the phone down in front of Lilli without further comment. "I got that yesterday from the police archives." He winked at her.

For the first time, Lilli saw a photograph of her father-in-law who had broken Klemens' heart by avoiding any contact with his son.

He had a sympathetic face, and Klemens was definitely his son: Galli's hair, his eyes and nose strikingly resembled those of her husband. Had the two of them ever met? In the photograph, Galli was smoking a cigarette and talking with a policeman. Alberti pointed to the man in uniform and said: "He was the first victim."

"Will you send the picture to my smartphone?"

"If you want." Alberti couldn't quite hide his surprise.

"Did you know that he was in the psychiatric clinic at the Ospedale Umberto I.?"

She shook her head.

"The dismissal from the police had ruined his life."

Lilli still hadn't gotten used to the heart pattern on his shirt. She wasn't sure if he really had as much heart, or none at all.

"It's a complicated case . . ." Alberti concluded.

Just then, Nicole returned, and her father interrupted their conversation, sent her the photo, and explained to his daughter that Lilli would take her to the evening of magic, and her mother would pick her up afterwards from the Hotel Excelsior.

An hour later, they said their goodbyes.

Nicole took Struppi (who had been sleeping the entire time under the table) and put him on his leash, took Lilli's hand, and they strolled down the Corso del Popolo. Time after time Nicole would stop and whisper to Lilli—apparently out of habit—as she pointed out disabled people. Without asking Lilli's permission, she would then approach them and smile at them, while Struppi wagged his tail and barked excitedly. There was a woman in a wheelchair, elegantly dressed with a jewelry chain. Her skin was whiter than that of anyone Lilli had ever seen. Her face was marred by illness, and her gaze revealed that she was in another reality. Nicole spontaneously asked Lilli for some money, disappeared with Struppi into a shop, came back with two bags of candy, and gave one to the woman. Lilli was taken by surprise. Just then, a young woman on a bike rode by, a baby in the basket on the handlebars, a small boy on the cargo rack, a girl on roller skates kept pace, talking with her mother as they went. Swallows circled the church tower of the Chiesa di San Giacomo.

When two school groups went past, several African children among them, Nicole's bag of candy was quickly emptied and Struppi had been petted by a dozen children. But at almost the same time, Nicole discovered an overweight severely-disabled child, wearing a crash helmet. Lilli thought it was probably an epileptic . . . She was so obese that she barely fit in her chair, her head was lowered, her eyes fixed on the tabletop.

In behavior, Klemens resembled Nicole, Lilli thought, of course he only approached the disabled when the situation arose or when they needed assistance. And then she suddenly understood that Klemens—since he felt cheated out of his childhood—reinvented it his whole life long. In his mind, there were parallel worlds that eventually replaced reality. What he had drawn and written were extracts from the Milky Way of his imagination . . .

At that moment, Nicole put a bottle of Coke Lite down beside the girl in the crash helmet and stroked her cheek, while Lilli paid their bill and Struppi sat by the table, attentively watching the activity.

"It's sweet of you to take me and Struppi to the Hotel Excelsior!" Nicole said in fragmentary Italian, as she and Lilli strolled along. She beamed at Lilli, pulled her down to her, and kissed her on the cheek.

Lilli smiled and gave her a ten-euro bill, before she put her money purse away. Nicole had started to eat some candy and laughed. A little further on, they came to a florist shop with potted plants on the sidewalk out front. Nicole instantly wanted to buy flowers for Lilli and had already opened the shop door, but Lilli was able to restrain her.

This was their routine as they approached the vaporetto station and stopped at the end of the Corso del Popolo by a market stall, since Lilli was debating whether to buy a polished mother-of-pearl shell for her bathroom. But while she was looking around, Nicole had bought a large cone shell and two smaller ones for eleven euros, and the woman behind the counter pointed out that she was one euro short. Lilli put the shells, already wrapped, into her bag and thanked Nicole who warily studied her to see if she was truly happy. Then she laughed heartily.

A red bicycle trailer in the form of a small ship's prow was parked at the vaporetto station. A childishly drawn yellow St. Mark's lion with halo, long beard and Bible was displayed on the side, under a white border and the black lettering: ULISSE. Lilli thought that Klemens would definitely have depicted the cart in one of his comics. Nicole raised her arm and pointed to it, shouting: "San Marco!" while Struppi raised a leg and peed on one of its tires.

They found seats in the vaporetto waiting platform as two women, roughly in their 40s with heads like birds, entered in the company of a nurse and sat down beside them. Nicole—absentmindedly petting Struppi—began a conversation with them. Lilli didn't understand a word, but they were polite with each other. She knew that the women's appearance was the consequence of a microcephaly, caused by rubella or the Zika virus during pregnancy, because Klemens had been fascinated by the movie *Freaks* that takes place in a circus where disabled artists appear and are displayed as attractions, and he had wanted to know what disease they had contracted. And, to be honest, the two women looked exactly like "Schlitzie," the assistant clown in the circus movie whose affliction Klemens had learned in conversation with a doctor.

The two women rarely spoke, but Nicole was apparently delighted when they merely nodded their heads.

When she heard the loud squawking of the seagulls, Lilli gazed out the window. A high-seas cutter was slowly sailing past on the left side of the vaporetto, it was white and accompanied by a thick swarm of gulls, because the highly perishable prawns had to be boiled on board and their remains were then tossed into the water to the delight of the gulls. The marine life was caught in nets that were lowered into the water by two beam trawls on the ship's stern. Lilli's father had owned a boat in Hamburg, that's why she knew so much about this method of fishing.

She was distracted by the sight of the gull mob, thinking about her little mosaic stone, about God, Klemens and his father, and Aldrian, the magician, in the Hotel Excelsior. After the cutter with its gulls had passed, she moved to a bench with a view of the landward side. Nicole was still scratching Struppi's head as the dog sat beside her, and the two women bent down and smiled at him. Presumably they were talking about the dog at that moment.

Before Lilli was swamped with more memories, she turned once again to the view from the window and saw a large family riding down the narrow bike path below the murazzi. Then, on the wall high above, she saw two old men looking out at the ocean. They sat there as if they might fish, but they had no fishing rods. Later, her gaze moved back to Nicole who, like the two women, was dozing off, while Struppi slept at her feet. She was glad that she had met Guido Alberti's daughter and her dog—because Klemens had also met them. She remembered that in one of their telephone conversations, he had spoken about "trisomy 21," the more recent terminology for Down syndrome. "They are not disabled," he had said, "they just have one chromosome too many . . . I have 46, and they have 47 . . ." He had told her much more about it, but now was not the time for her to relive her memories, she preferred to look out the window.

The vaporetto moved past a shipwreck that lay on its side in the water at the shoreline. It was yellow, the deck white, and the hull blue. Then two men—one in swimming trunks, the other in running shoes, gym shorts and T-shirt—jogged along the wall above the shore. She knew nothing about them, and they knew nothing about her. They weren't even men, she corrected herself, they were the clock hands of time that was running out on her . . .

The two disabled women got off at the vaporetto's last stop and said goodbye to Nicole and Struppi.

As they crossed the island of Pellestrina on the bus, Lilli only looked at the stone blocks of the wall. She didn't exactly know what was behind it, she didn't know what to expect. Nicole sat across from her and held Struppi in her lap. She seemed to be lost in thought. Should she pay Alberti's daughter a compliment? Lilli wondered. Pet the dog?—The speeding bus jostled its passengers and made several stops. Nicole gazed sleepily at her watch and suddenly beamed. It was 5 o'clock. The show would start in just one hour.

7

The Magician in the Hotel Excelsior

The remainder of the ride to the Hotel Excelsior, Nicole pressed her face against the window as if, at the last stop, she would be quizzed on whether she had seen every single thing, Lilli thought.

On the lagoon side, a bridge crossed a canal that led directly to the Excelsior, which was ahead of them. They got off the bus, relieved that they had escaped the bus's jouncing. A motorboat was delivering guests who all seemed to be excited about the evening of magic. Some looked around happily, others expectantly at the hotel. Nicole stopped to wave, and all the passengers on deck waved back. Lilli couldn't help embracing Nicole. They hugged, and Lilli almost cried, though she didn't know why.

They were expected in the Excelsior's convention center. The entire hotel was draped in white—the walls, the leather armchairs, all the other furnishings—the large chandelier that hung from the ceiling as well, as well as abundant floral decorations. Other children were already racing around, and teenagers stood around in groups. Nicole went right over to them, keeping her dog on a short leash. To Lilli's amazement, Struppi didn't bark.

From the outset she didn't understand a single word of the entertainment—at first, she really made an effort, but then she just began to enjoy the situation. She felt as if she were reliving her school days. Soon all the guests were assembled. A door opened and a white angel with oversized wings appeared, accompanied by a clown pushing a flower cart and placing garlands on the girls' heads or yellow baseball caps on the boys. During the ensuing commotion, a brass band in fancy uniforms formed up and threw confetti on the audience. It was like a blizzard of colorful snow. Then the musicians began to play a turbulent piece until the children had halfway calmed down. Now the angel stepped up, greeted the audience with exaggerated gestures, while the clown made mute faces. Lilli still didn't understand a word, but since the children were clapping and laughing, she assumed that the speech was witty. With a drum roll and trumpet fanfare, the magician, dressed as an old man, came onstage, bowed and removed his top hat, revealing white mice. He put the top hat back on, and when he took it in his hands and bowed again, two doves were ensconced in his hair as if they had just hatched eggs. They flew off as the children howled, landing on the large stately chandeliers and on the angel's head. The magician was undoubtedly Aldrian. Meanwhile he plucked more small white balls in the shape of doves' eggs from his sleeve and began to juggle them. There were more and more balls, the band played faster and faster—finally the magician tossed all the eggs up into the air and the clown deftly caught them, distributed them to the audience, and asked the children and teenagers to open them. In each of the white balls was a slip of paper with a number, Lilli supposed they were lottery tickets. In the meantime, Aldrian had started to do card tricks, he asked questions, gave suggestions, and made everybody laugh with his humorous answers. In closing, to a drum roll and wild applause, he threw the cards through the window pane without breaking it, and they disintegrated outside in mid-air. Lilli had never seen this trick before . . . And already the magician was speaking of poisonous snakes that were supposedly trying to get into the hotel, as colored paper snakes fell from the ceiling, causing the audience to shriek and then burst out laughing. Without an announcement, it turned dark, and seconds later the magician appeared, first as Donald Duck, then as Mickey Mouse, as Goofy, and then back as a magician, no longer in the guise of an old man, but as the White Rabbit from *Alice in Wonderland*. He gave a sign, and hotel employees instantly rushed in with tables and chairs, the band played "Azzurro," and the children all sang along. Aldrian gave another sign, the tables were set, the band now played "La Paloma," and doves were released from the chandeliers, landing on the magician's shoulders, and before the food and drinks were served, an Italian march was played that sounded very festive.

The seats at the tables were distributed according to the number on each ticket, so that Lilli was seated next to Nicole who ate her spaghetti with great gusto. The guests could choose between spaghetti Bolognese and pizza, but the high point of the festivities wasn't reached until the desert was served—ice cream, cake, and fruit. Aldrian had left the stage some time ago and was mingling among the children, along with the clown and the angel. Meanwhile, the band played their showpiece, "O sole mio."

For the first time, Lilli felt something akin to happiness. Later the audience drank lemonade, juices, mineral water, and Coke; Nicole's mother, Lisa, a likeable woman, arrived. Alberti had apparently told her over the phone who Lilli was . . . Lisa thanked her effusively that she had taken such good care of her daughter. She spoke perfect English which was no surprise since she—as Lilli learned—had taught English before her marriage at a high school. In the course of their conversation, Lisa explained that this evening's sponsor was a foundation called *MORNING*, financed by Signor Egon Blanc. Lilli remembered the message she had received last night in the porter's lodge. In it, some South Tyrolean named Lanz had communicated an invitation from a Signor Blanc. And she immediately thought of the murder of the policeman at the Bacino and the photograph of the former Commissario Galli.

"You don't need to be concerned," Lisa was saying, as if she could read Lilli's mind. "Signor Lanz is our angel today, and Aldrian's wife is playing the clown, while Aldrian himself is, of course, the magician . . . Lanz and Aldrian are from Vienna, their wives are Italian . . ."

"And Signor Blanc?"

"Signor Blanc is about a hundred years old. He speaks more than ten languages fluently, and, aside from persistent fatigue, is still mentally sharp."

Lilli watched the children and teenagers and now felt she belonged with them, though she still knew that it was only a hope of escaping her pain and her sorrow.

Their conversation was interrupted, as the raffle was about to begin. Each of the children could read the number on their ticket, while the magician drew the winning numbers from the imitation dove eggs, and the clown handed out the prizes. Since all the children had received a bag of confetti along with their presents, a constant swirl of colorful paper flakes rained down, their spirits were sky-high. Now Struppi could no longer hold back and started barking—Lisa had to take him outside.

Absurdly enough, in addition to the lottery drawing, there was an iPad for each child and teenager, resulting in horrendous cheering. When one of the iPads, gift-wrapped with a big silk bow, was handed out, the band played "Happy Birthday," and everyone sang along.

When it got dark, the crowd of guests went out onto the terrace where a fantastic fireworks display lit up the sky above the dark waters. After three hours, the party was over. With Nicole and Struppi in hand, Lisa said goodbye. They had learned that motorboats would return them all to St. Mark's Square.

Lilli felt tired and wanted to leave, too, but the magician, still in full make-up, introduced the "angel" who was already back in street clothes.

"I didn't expect to see you here," the South Tyrolean Lanz greeted Lilli and introduced himself. She shook hands with him, wondering how she could get out of here as soon as possible.

"I've read your husband's work," Lanz continued, "and think very highly of it—the early work as well as the most recent . . ."

Lilli nodded.

". . . time and again I decided to translate something of his into Italian or English, but then I discovered that it had already been done."

"You're a translator?" Lilli asked, even though the porter had already mentioned it. He nodded and invited her to join him in the hotel restaurant. Lilli replied that she had already eaten pizza with the children, so he suggested they have a glass of wine—Michael Aldrian and his wife Beatrice would join them, he added.

In the course of the next two hours, she learned that Lanz was in the process of translating William Shakespeare's complete works into Italian, and that Signor Blanc was a paradox: a famous man that no one knew, who read everything. He was even knowledgeable about her late husband's comics, the translator emphasized. Blanc had an urgent request to meet her.

That was presumably the reason why the "magician" (as she secretly called Aldrian) invited her and why the "angel" had left the message in the Hotel Diana. Ultimately Lilli wanted to know who told Lanz that she was staying in Venice? Was it Herr Aldrian?

"Signor Blanc runs a computer center where all relevant information is evaluated," was the reply. Aldrian stated that he would gladly give her more details, but not here. However, Lanz dangled an invitation for the weekend to the island of Sant'Erasmo where she could meet Egon Blanc in person. And Aldrian added: "But, at best, you'll only get to see his back. He doesn't want to be recognized."

Lilli changed the subject and asked Aldrian if he knew the former Police Inspector Galli.

The answer was laughter: "What about Galli?" they asked her. But Lilli didn't explain. All three had already had their "experiences" (as they called it) with him. He was a remarkably rational man, a kind of Sherlock Holmes, according to Lanz. "He believes he can explain the entire world, and doesn't recognize that all abilities are limited. According to legend, he often solved criminal cases that he had only read about in newspapers, even before the interrogation of the suspects, though he failed in two cases where he had supposedly uncovered everything, because he wasn't able to convince his superiors with his evidence."

"He lost his nerve," Lanz continued. "That's the reason he was initially suspended and ultimately dismissed."

Lanz, Aldrian, and his wife took Lilli in a white private motorboat back to the Piazzetta where they said their cordial farewells.

"Are you religious?" Beatrice asked unexpectedly, before they got back in the boat.

"Why do you ask?" Lilli replied, astonished.

"There are so many churches and religious paintings in Venice."

To her surprise Lilli answered with what she had long felt, but never put into words: "I don't like discussions about God. Anything you might say is trivial . . ."

Beatrice nodded and smiled: "So, no?"

Lilli shook her head. ". . . it's just that I'm probably too religious for religion," she said, also smiling.

She felt wide-awake.

In the hotel room, even before she turned on the lights, she walked over to the window. There were still a few people sitting at tables in the open-air restaurant. She thought about Nicole and Struppi and the magic evening in the Hotel Excelsior, then swallowed one of the sleeping pills she had taken from Aldrian's suitcase, lay down on the bed, and fell asleep—her final thought—like "Little Nemo."

8
The Latest News

She dreamed that the earth was no bigger than a walnut. The people were so small that they were only detectable as tiny dots in an electron microscope. Lilli was just observing a swarm of dots through the lens and asked herself what laws held them together. She had often seen that two particles had united, resulting in a third, even smaller particle; but also, after the union, one of the two dots disappeared. She was about to put the walnut under the microscope so she could see more, when she heard ringing. And when she woke up, she realized that it was the room telephone and that she would never see the walnut again.

"Commissario Zacchini . . . Sorry if I woke you, I've got to speak with you!"

She glanced at her wristwatch on the nightstand—it was already 9:30, the sun was shining outside, but Lilli was still woozy.

"Yes, why?" she heard herself ask.

"I'll be there in half-an-hour." He hung up without saying goodbye.

Suddenly, Lilli was wide-awake, she hurried to take a shower and put on her makeup.

On the one hand, she had no idea what the inspector wanted from her, on the other, she was trying to remember what had happened to the walnut in her dream.

In front of the mirror, she diverted her attention with thoughts of the children and teenagers in the Hotel Excelsior. She thought of the two organizers of the children's party, Aldrian and Lanz, and that she could ask one of them to be with her during her conversation with the inspector, to translate his questions and her answers . . . She decided on Lanz since he had claimed to be a translator. She had barely slipped into her dress, when there was a knock at the door.

Inspector Luca Zacchini looked exhausted, he coughed, and asked if he might come in. He was followed by a policeman and two men who introduced themselves as his assistant Perlucci and his interpreter Gamper, whose name hinted that he, too, was from South Tyrol. Since there were only two chairs in the room, the policeman went back out into the hallway, while Perlucci and Gamper sat down on the bed. It was silent for several minutes. First, the inspector explained that Guido Alberti had been murdered and his body had been found three hours ago at the final stop of bus Line #11 on Pellestrina, his throat slit and his eyes gouged out. Lilli had to brace herself so that she didn't fall apart. The longer the session lasted, the more often she saw a picture of his corpse in the shirt with the heart design and gouged-out eyes. She was relieved that the inspector's questions and her answers were being translated since pauses occurred that allowed her to prepare herself for the ensuing questions. It also gave her an opportunity to observe the inspector's face and his reactions to her answers or, from some of the Italian words she recognized, to anticipate subsequent questions or objections. When Nicole's name came up, she had to reach for a tissue from the package on the desk to dry her eyes. That all took place in the tense silence in the room.

She was thoroughly questioned about the encounter with Alberti and his daughter in the furniture store, why she had gone there, what could have persuaded Klemens to stay there, the trip to Chioggia, and their lunch in the Osteria Penzo.

She explained in detail that Alberti had been on the trail of Francesco Galli whose girlfriend lived in a house across from the Osteria, and that Alberti had been waiting for him.

"And then what?" Zacchini asked.

"Then I went with Nicole to a party in the Hotel Excelsior."

"Yes, that's what Lisa Alberti said. And afterwards?"

She told about the white motorboat, about Aldrian, his wife, and about Lanz.

"What made you think of Francesco Galli when we first spoke?"

"Have you arrested him?"

"No, he's not in Chioggia, not in his apartment on Pellestrina, and not in Padua. He's vanished into thin air."

At first Lilli hesitated to tell Zacchini everything. But then she thought it was best to share her search for the father of her late husband.

"Was that the reason why your husband was in Venice?" Zacchini abruptly asked, as if he were trying to trip her up.

"He was here because of his work. Just before he left on this last trip, he learned who his actual father was and had begun to look for him."

The inspector thought for a moment.

"I would advise you not to undertake anything on your own initiative," he then said. "If you do, you'll be in danger . . . We've learned that in the last several years, Galli's been living in Cannaregio."

"Near the Madonna dell'Orto church?"

"Yes, why do you ask?"

"Klemens liked that church. And the painter Tintoretto is buried there."

Zacchini considered that fact.

"Do you think that your husband met Galli in the church?"

"No, it wasn't until shortly before he left for Venice that Klemens learned from his mother that he was Galli's son, and from the drawings he made, he wasn't in Cannaregio."

"He may not have drawn everything he did or saw."

Lilli shrugged her shoulders.

"Let's assume he met him. What would have happened after that?"

"He would have kept it to himself." Once again, she saw Alberti in his shirt with the heart pattern, the bloody eye-sockets, and Nicole and Struppi.

"Why are you so sure?"

She waited until her thoughts had calmed down. Then she remembered her suspicion that Klemens had a lover, so she felt it was better if she didn't respond to the inspector's questions. "I'm sorry, I've told you everything," was her answer.

"And I'm sorry that I have to ask you these questions. I know it's difficult for you to have to think about all this . . . But I do have one more question I'd like to ask: Did the suspect you saw at the killing in the Bacino have a resemblance to your husband?"

"Why would you think that?" Lilli countered.

"I mean, if your husband looked like Francesco Galli, then you must have noticed that . . . For example, how he moved, the shape of his head, his hair . . . ?"

"No, everything happened so fast that I don't even know if I really saw what I think I remember, or if it's just my imagination."

Again, Zacchini paused to think.

"I understand," he then said. "But why did your husband go to Padua, to Pellestrina and Chioggia? Do you have an explanation? Those are places where Francesco Galli lived. Your husband must even have known about the girlfriend across from the Osteria, about his residences—that means he knew for certain where to look for Galli and perhaps have met him, too."

"What does that have to do with the police killings? Why would Commissario Galli have murdered people who had precisely the same profession as he previously did?"

"Out of revenge for his dismissal . . . for the loss of his job and his reputation and, not least of all, the meaning of his life."

Lilli closed her eyes, lowered her head, and was silent. But Zacchini was waiting for her answer, and the longer she remained silent, the harder it would be for her to say anything plausible.

"You would know that better than I do," she finally responded.

Zacchini didn't let on what he thought of her last answer, it seemed as if he was thinking hard again.

"Fine," he said, stood up, said goodbye, then stopped in the doorway and apprehensively told her that she shouldn't, under any circumstances, investigate on her own. "If anything occurs to you, call me! I'm here for you. Will you promise me that?"

"Yes."

His assistant Perlucci hadn't said a word the entire time, only Gamper had translated.

Lilli still couldn't believe that Alberti was dead. And Nicole? Had they already told her about the news?

She lay back down on the bed and closed her eyes. Finally, she took her phone out of her bag and Alberti's business card from her money purse, took a deep breath, and dialed his number. It occurred to her that the police must be in possession of his smartphone, and she ended the call before she heard the dial tone. Instead, she called the number of the furniture store, but no one answered. For a time, she just lay there with her eyes closed, but she immediately opened them again when the image of the murdered Guido Alberti came to mind.

Early that afternoon she had gnocchi brought up to her room and ate the meal apathetically.

She was actually hungry for justice, she thought . . . that just occurred to her when she was obsessed with something else. Her thoughts were still with Alberti, Nicole, her mother Lisa, and Struppi the dog. Now she knew why no one at the furniture store had answered the phone . . . A couple of days ago she was in the same predicament, and she had eventually fled . . . Just like former Inspector Galli . . . Now she simply had to know if Klemens had met him . . . And she wanted to conclude Klemens' search for his father . . . She wouldn't be able to leave Venice until she had found out what he had been doing these past few weeks . . . Under no circumstances would she return to Vienna. When she thought about the everyday routine she would be subjected to, she panicked. She also didn't want to be with people who pitied her, and even less with those who long ago had resumed their old routines. The only thing that attracted her was a return to the Kunsthistorisches Museum, to walk through the galleries with the paintings that, as she thought about it, she had already seen thousands of times. They were, she felt, her actual world, no longer her secondary one, as before. Instead, the daily routine had now become her secondary reality, it seemed like a nightmare where she was vulnerable to all those events that bombarded her without letup. Klemens' fate bothered her most of all. And she felt she owed it to herself to clear up the puzzling events.

She had taken sleeping pills to calm down, but the decision to stay in Venice until everything was solved was cathartic. Her other intention was to confront circumstances as they existed. This thought also calmed her. And she had to take time for what she really wanted.

She didn't have to think long, because she was aware that she could prowl around Venice, doing whatever she had in mind. It was all about the present day, and no one could expect her to justify herself.

And she would have to change hotels, this place constantly reminded her of Klemens. She decided to act spontaneously and leave things to chance. First, however, she wanted to see the bridge where Klemens had died.

In the meantime, the sky had grown dark. She took the thin black windbreaker with hood out of her suitcase, remembered to put in the new sunglasses case with the little mosaic stone, and packed her sunglasses into her purse, checked that her smartphone was turned off and automatically put it in the pocket of her windbreaker. Last of all, she put her money purse in the inner pocket of her windbreaker and zipped it shut.

Since Alberti's murder, she felt something like a growing resistance to everything.

Ignoring everything else, she left the hotel, took a side street and passed by a pharmacy near St. Mark's that had a life-size skeleton in its display window. It didn't matter to her if it was real or synthetic, but now she imagined all the tourists and vendors on the Square as skeletons in street clothes. She thought Klemens would have found that amusing. The market stalls at the Giardinetti were offering selfie sticks and small colored plastic busts of world-famous soccer players. At one point, Klemens thought he would buy one of the Argentine and Barcelona star Messi, since they both had the same birthday. He secretly bought the statue the following day and, back at the hotel, put it in bed with her and had a good laugh. She had never really understood that he could make such a big deal about his childhood.

While waiting for the vaporetto, she saw a group of South American tourists, men and women taking pictures of each other. They happily leaped into the air, stretched out their arms, then whirled in a circle, laughing loudly as they were being photographed, subsequently performing a group hug.

In the Line #1 vaporetto that went to the train station, the only available seats were in front of Arabic-looking teenagers who had their feet on the backs of the seats ahead of them. They were wearing sneakers, two of them had hoodies, but she still sat down on one of the plastic seats. The vaporetto cast off, and she immediately felt shoes pressing against her buttocks. And sure enough, the teens didn't speak Italian with each other, but Arabic. When another seat became free before the next stop, she changed to the opposite side of the ship. The first raindrops began to fall from the dark sky. She could see through the window that the city was immersed in a dull grey light and the water of the Lagoon had turned deep-green. The vaporetto swayed, groaning, from station to station, more and more passengers boarded with luggage on their way to the train station. Before they arrived at the Rialto stop, it began to rain. Lilli saw the drops on the water. And then the ship was struck by an avalanche of people, though only some were allowed to board. Now it was really pouring, and at all the remaining stops to the train station the chaos was repeated.

At the final stop of Ferrovia, Lilli waited until most of the passengers had gotten off. She was still angry at the provocative behavior of the Arabic boys who were nowhere to be seen.

It had stopped raining, but the sky was still dark.

She quickly reached the Ponte degli Scalzi, the bridge where Klemens had suffered his fatal injuries. The stone structure was large and spanned the Grand Canal. Lilli crossed the bridge, thought about Klemens, and silently spoke to him: "I love you," she said. She didn't hear an answer, and, strangely enough, felt nothing as she went down the other side. She had secretly been afraid of what she might encounter, but now she saw only stones and steps, and felt relieved as she headed off in the direction of the Jewish Ghetto. Obviously wondering where he had fallen, she looked down and studied the steps, but shoes incessantly tromped past her, large and small ones, loafers and walking shoes.

For her it was like a parable about dying and being forgotten. For a moment she felt disconnected from the people, disconnected from the passage of time, but she didn't allow other feelings to surface. She felt she now had the hardest part behind her. She didn't intend to visit the Ghetto—she had already visited the synagogues three or four times with Klemens—she would much rather go to Cannaregio and the Madonna dell'Orto church and to the Ospedale Umberto I. with its asilo that her husband had mentioned so often. Someone there possibly knew Francesco Galli, if he really had stayed there. She took the city map out of her jacket, unfolded it to orient herself, and just as Lilli was refolding the map, an unfamiliar woman spoke to her, asking if she could be of help. She was about forty years old, well-groomed, and cordial.

"Do you speak Italian?" the woman asked, and when Lilli shook her head, the stranger began to speak English, asking where Lilli came from. Lilli explained that she wanted to visit the Madonna dell'Orto church. The woman began to speak about Tintoretto who was buried there, but Lilli interrupted her and assured her that she knew all about the painter, the Kunsthistorisches Museum in Vienna had a large number of amazing pictures by him: portraits of bearded men, *Susanna Bathing*, *King Belshazzar's Banquet* . . .

"Oh, are you an art historian?"

"Yes. And you?"

"I'm a tour guide . . . I studied languages, got married, dropped out of the university, and was suddenly alone . . . So, I did the next best thing . . ."

They began to walk faster, didn't speak as they arrived at the Campo San Geremia, and from there, the bridge over the Canale di Cannaregio. Lilli, who had regained her bearings, stopped and thanked the woman, but, to her surprise, heard the woman offer to accompany her. Lilli was torn—she really wanted to be alone, but it was better if the guide came along to interpret, in case the opportunity arose to inquire about Francesco Galli. But if she should unexpectedly bump into the Commissario, she thought, it would be dangerous, since the woman might possibly inform on her to the police.

Ultimately, she asked her companion to just show her the way. The woman handed her a business card, in case she ever wanted to do a tour of the city, pointed straight ahead, briefly waved, and hurried off.

Since it had begun to rain again, Lilli pulled the hood over her head, came to the Campo Ghetto Nuovo, and walked alongside it to the bridge over the Rio di San Girolamo.

She liked the area with its low tile houses and the canals and small tributaries. She had the impression of sharing something of the lives of people in the city. Actually, she had always wanted to live in Venice . . . It rained harder, she crossed two more bridges, and finally stood before the white plastered building with its closed shutters that she assumed was the Sant'Alvise convent. A man was sitting on the steps at the entrance to the church, eating something. He wasn't poorly dressed.

She pulled the hood tightly over her head before she came closer. She immediately realized that the man had a bottle in a brown paper bag beside him, and, when he thought no one was watching, would take a drink. Then he put the bottle in the paper bag back on the step.

Lilli was alert. She especially enjoyed seeing the canal and the tile buildings. However, each time she gazed at the convent and the church, she noticed that the man had just put his bottle back down.

The rain quit just as abruptly as it had started. She herself knew how alcohol made every bleak corner more bearable—she felt sorry for the man. So, she took out her money purse, looked for a 20-euro bill, and approached the man who lurched up, clutched his bottle, and was apparently going to run off. But with several rapid steps, Lilli caught up with him and handed him the banknote. He hesitated and said something in an unfriendly tone that she didn't understand. She had a sudden inspiration, took out her smartphone, looked for the photograph of Francesco Galli, and held it up for the man to see.

The man stopped. "Police?" he asked, derisively.

Lilli shook her head.

"Io sono . . ." she hesitated, because she didn't know the Italian words for 'father-in-law' or for 'daughter-in-law,' but she remembered that the Latin word for 'daughter' was *filia*. "Filia," she said, and again held the smartphone up for him.

"Commissario . . ." the man blurted out, hesitantly. And again: "Commissario . . ." He turned around without taking the money.

"Nomen Commissario?" Lilli asked, again using the Latin word.

"Nomi?" the man corrected.

"Si, nomi . . . Commissario?"

He turned back to face her, took the money, blurted out "Galli," turned away, and ran off. Without looking back, he stretched out his arm twice and pointed in the direction of the sea. Lilli once again consulted her map and learned that the building in the distance was the former Ospedale Umberto I. and a psychiatric clinic. She headed in that direction until she came to a main door that had a handwritten white cardboard sign that read "Asilo," "Homeless Shelter." A two-way intercom system and a series of doorbell buttons without names were mounted on a tile column, but since she didn't speak Italian, she entered the courtyard without ringing. She had almost overlooked the glass wall to her right with the sign: "Concierge." The long counter was deserted. The white corridor she had passed through was, when she looked back, also empty. In the courtyard she encountered two locked doors and a sign warning her to keep out. Lilli looked through a glass pane in the door and saw a lovely garden with a meadow, shrubs, trees, and blossoming forsythia, and in the distance, a yellow building . . . washing was hanging from a window to dry. So, someone must be living there. She now saw other long yellow buildings that gave the impression of being abandoned.

She was just about to turn around when a heavy-set man in jeans and a vest with a pony tail appeared, heading in her direction. He approached the doorbell resolutely, asked the intercom to be let in, hurried across the courtyard where he shoved open the now-unlocked second door, and waited until Lilli had caught up with him. With the hood partially covering her face (though it had stopped raining), she acted as if she knew which building she was looking for.

She came to an overgrown garden landscape with tall grass, trees, and nettles—and, unexpectedly, a short section of asphalt that led outside the park. She read a sign with the inscription "ASILO," and noticed outside the typically yellow building, swings, slides, monkey bars, and a large sandbox. She paused and looked on her smartphone for the translation of "asilo." Amazed, she learned that the word also meant "kindergarten." What was Klemens in a kindergarten? At first, she thought it had to do with the homeless shelter. She assumed he had either come here by accident or had met someone at this out-of-the-way place. In any case, he had been here twice, according to his notes. She thought long and hard about this dilemma when she heard noise not far off, behind the next building, clearly coming from children.

After she had passed the building, the former park opened to a view of a well-tended garden and an arbor with benches. Further off, toward the ocean, she saw a bunker that apparently came from the time when Venice belonged to the Habsburg Empire. She then saw little children running from the beach to the benches, yelling and dancing, as if they were playing tag. Following them, also laughing, were young women—presumably the kindergarten teachers. A little later, an older woman in a white smock appeared—probably the principal, she assumed. Lilli slowly approached the area, because the children had now begun to sing and to sit on the benches. It was a happy song, but Lilli suddenly felt like an abandoned child. She abruptly turned away, took out one of the tissues that she always kept in her jacket, wiped her eyes, composed herself, put the handkerchief back, and approached the older woman, determined, almost angry—though she didn't know why. The woman stopped, apparently trying to decide who Lilli was, couldn't come up with an answer, and tried to put on a strict expression.

"Do you speak English?" Lilli asked, as she was still a few steps away.

The woman nodded and continued to observe her with a stern expression.

At that moment Lilli didn't know what she wanted to say.

She stammered something and immediately began to sob, and the older woman touched her arm and gently led her into the one-story building where the children presumably sought shelter from the heat or rain. Toys lay on the floor, a piano stood against the wall beside a bookcase, the window was open, and the glass pane reflected the agitated image of dark rainclouds and the grey-green ocean with small waves.

Lilli apologized. Still fighting tears, she explained to her escort that her husband had died and only recently been buried.

The woman nodded. Her stern expression had disappeared, and she now displayed sympathy.

"I'm looking for Francesco Galli," she blurted out.

The woman's expression became cautious, and Lilli heard her say firmly that she didn't know any Galli.

"My husband had searched for him without success . . . Galli is his father," Lilli replied solemnly.

She again took out a tissue and gradually calmed down.

"I've come to tell him about his son's death."

The woman tried to give an impression of impartiality, but Lilli noticed that she was struggling with something.

"I'm not from the police," Lilli continued. She took out her money purse and showed the woman her driver's license.

Lilli fell silent, and the woman in the white smock also said nothing. Through the open window, they could hear the children singing, which made Lilli tear up again. She couldn't hold back her tears and said, as she took out another tissue from her jacket: "Now everything's coming out . . ."

"Who was your husband?" the woman asked politely in a calm voice.

"His name was Klemens Kuck. At our wedding he took my name, Kuck, because he wanted to discard the name of his adoptive parents. He had had a difficult childhood. As he grew older, he began to draw comic books, and initially published comics for children."

"We have his comics in our asilo."

She stepped over to the bookcase by the piano, bent down, and pulled out two worn-out copies. Lilli had to turn away, because Klemens was suddenly as close as at any time since his death. It seemed to her as if he had been hiding in this kindergarten, and she now felt that he was nearby.

"Why are you looking for Signor . . . Galli . . . and here, of all places? He could be somewhere else in Venice . . . I mean, do you have some indication that he is staying with us?"

"No, but I heard that he was treated for depression at the Ospedale Umberto I. for a time."

"And that is why you have come to the kindergarten?"

Lilli gave a straightforward answer: "My husband was supposedly here in Venice, searching for his father, when a stranger pushed him down the steps of the Ponte degli Scalzi and he suffered fatal injuries."

She hadn't noticed that one of the two young teachers had come into the room.

"Is everything okay, Mama?" she asked in Italian.

Since Lilli only understood the word "Mama," she suspected

that this was the daughter of the kindergarten principal. Lilli understood that the mother was trying to shoo her away, but the young woman butted in and finally took the cellphone out of her jeans pocket. She had a brief conversation and, as Lilli went to the door because she realized the senselessness of her effort, the young teacher made an animated gesture: she should wait.

"He's coming," the mother said in English without emotion, avoiding looking at Lilli.

Just then the daughter's phone rang. The conversation didn't last long, then the young teacher took Lilli by the arm and explained that she should come along with her. Francesco was on the beach, but he didn't live here, he lived elsewhere . . .

They went past the singing, laughing children, down to the bunker where the young woman stopped and pointed out a man with his back to them, staring out to sea. Without another word the teacher silently turned back, as Lilli cautiously approached the figure. The ocean slapped the shore. In the distance she could hear a vaporetto chugging along and the omnipresent loud squawking of the gulls in the grey sky.

When the man turned around, she recognized the familiar features of her Klemens.

They faced each other in silence, until Galli nodded, came over, and shook her hand. He immediately turned back to face the sea and said, as if to himself: "My son is dead?"

Lilli was surprised at herself—her fear was suddenly gone, the tears, the sorrow, the uncertainty. Actually, she just wanted to accuse Galli of how shabbily he had treated his son and his wife when he deserted them, and that Klemens had only died because he had been searching for his father, but she restrained herself.

"You must hate me, I expect that," Galli said in English. "Maybe you'll tell the police that you've found me, maybe you'll shout it out . . ."

"It was a series of events that led me to you," Lilli answered.

"You were his wife?"

Lilli nodded. Even though she hadn't intended to do it, she began to make accusations, told him how Klemens had died, everything Klemens had done to find his father, and how miserable his rural childhood had been.

"It would have been better if he hadn't been determined to find me . . ." Galli replied.

Even though he was nicely dressed, he looked drained. His grey hair was messed, he had a three-day-old beard, only the glasses and his sleepy eyes hinted at the brilliance of a keen intellect. And his green rain jacket over the black T-shirt and the beige-brown jeans suggested an earlier youthful charm.

"I was with Alberti and his daughter Nicole in the Osteria Penzo in Chioggia," Lilli said. "Signor Alberti had suddenly decided to wait for you by the Osteria and to speak with you—he insisted that you were living with your girlfriend in one of the buildings across the street. So, I rode alone with Nicole back to the Lido and went with her to the Hotel Excelsior where the Egon Blanc Foundation had arranged an evening for children with Down syndrome. The next morning the police came and informed me of Alberti's murder. They found his body in the water by the vaporetto station on Pellestrina, not far from your apartment. Before that, I was an inadvertent witness to the third police murder at the Bacino."

The ocean murmured, somewhere a ship's horn tooted, and seagulls still screeched under the dark sky. And you could still hear the asilo children singing in the distance.

"It would be better if you go now!" Galli softly responded. "You've told me everything . . . I've heard everything . . . I wasn't in Chioggia and wasn't on Pellestrina. I left my girlfriend two months ago, so Alberti couldn't have seen me there. I guess Guido, poor Guido, found the real killer . . ."

"And who would that be?"

"You came here just to ask me that?"

After a pause, Galli continued: "I loved my work with the police, I am still in contact with colleagues and know what's going on in my former beat . . . Yes, I still love the work . . ." He lapsed into silence.

She suddenly wanted to accuse him of despicable acts, because he hadn't said a word about Klemens. So, she asked him if he were indifferent to the fact that his son died while looking for him.

"You didn't visit him one single time during his childhood. And later on, you just disappeared!"

"Get out of my life!" Galli shouted at her. "As far as I'm concerned, my son has been dead for over forty years. I've forgotten him, do you understand? He no longer existed for me . . ." He fell silent and disappeared into the bunker.

Lilli briefly paused, then went back to the kindergarten, detoured around the building, and unexpectedly stood in front of the young teacher.

"It's my fault . . ." the woman said. "I shouldn't have taken you to Galli."

Lilli, too, stood there, thinking about how she should respond.

"For years Francesco has been in a severe crisis," the teacher continued. "He insists that Egon Blanc ruined him. And he says that people only see the good in Blanc. In reality, he is a criminal who eliminates everything that stands in his way and is indifferent to people's suffering."

Lilli dried her eyes.

"You are wrong if you suspect Francesco," the young teacher declared. "It was all about an unsolved criminal case involving Blanc. The billionaire Blanc ruined Galli. At his instigation, Galli was fired, and no one believed a word he said in his defense."

"Were you eavesdropping on us?" Lilli asked warily.

The young woman was silent and resolutely looked Lilli straight in the eye.

"Why is he hiding out with you?" Lilli wanted to know. Her voice was still full of suspicion.

"After his dismissal from the police force, he was admitted to a psychiatric clinic and treated. My mother was a nurse in the ward where he was assigned. When he was half-way recovered, he visited my mother who had taken over the kindergarten after her psychiatric practice dissolved." She paused. "Promise me that you will keep this to yourself?" she asked, in a compromising tone.

"No one will hear anything from me . . ."

"Go home. It's better for you . . . We're just helping a person who has fallen on hard times through no fault of his own!" She impulsively gave Lilli a hug, then tore herself away and ran off.

Lilli was so confused that, at first, she couldn't find her way back to the road.

In front of the Sant'Alvise convent there were boats in the canal where teenage boys—one with a fishing net in his hand—did acrobatics and yelled something to her that she didn't understand. They were roughly fifteen years old, Lilli estimated, and apparently were looking for trouble. So, she stared at the ground, but the tallest one—he wore a yellow pullover—shouted an obscenity (or so she concluded from his tone), while the others broke out in malicious laughter and kept repeating the expression. They also didn't stop when she crossed the next bridge. There wasn't a soul in sight. She now forced herself to imagine what she could do to regain her equilibrium. But had anything been normal over these past few weeks?

Walking along the canal, with homes on the left bank that seemed devoid of people, she came to the Madonna dell'Orto church . . . She opened the heavy entrance door and purchased a ticket from an elderly woman at the register. As she entered the nave and noticed that she was alone, she imagined a situation where there were no more believers in the whole world or that the entire city had become extinct. On the other hand, she found the silence soothing. Everything she had recently experienced seemed to have taken place in a parallel universe. It remained "outside." Here she found herself in the semi-darkness of a universe of myth and fable, of images and silence. She didn't have the strength for an inner discourse, there was too much inside her that was destroyed, but she found her place in the void of wordlessness, it was a chance for her to catch her breath, as if on a long hike. She paused at Tintoretto's *The Last Judgment* that reminded her of the mosaic in St. Mark's Basilica and of the little glass stone that she had in her purse. She couldn't identify with the meanings of the painting. And she recalled what the young teacher had said about Signor Blanc, but she suppressed her memories and concentrated on the pictures on the walls. The *Idolatry of Golden Calf* in a side chapel, on the other hand, seemed like a scene out of a cinemascope film by Stanley Kubrick. Clearly, Tintoretto had an extraordinary spatial imagination, as Lilli well knew. The painter was a fabulist whose temperament prevailed and whose vivid imagination allowed him to create scenes that could have come from comics five hundred years ago. In a letter from Venice a year ago, Klemens had outlined his opinion of Tintoretto: He was a church artist who, in the style of Catholic Realism had translated the *Biblia pauperum*—the Bible of the Poor who couldn't read—by making Holy Scripture visible in a brilliant way. She had remembered this description and felt it hit the mark. The painter let himself be swept along by his religious themes, she believed, and—although a great artist—he was unpredictable and popular and created dramatic evocative paintings, frequently employing deceptions of perspective. She turned to a side chapel that seemed as abandoned as she felt. As she knew, a pathetic empty gold frame hung there, below it a notice stating that the painting by Giovanni Bellini had been stolen "in March of 1993," and a photograph, crudely mounted on cardboard, illustrated the loss. The empty gold frame on the white wall now impressed Lilli more that she had expected. She understood it as an illustration of the absence of God. For a time, she stood there, starring at the gold-framed white patch of wall. It also matched her own situation that, together with the fast and furious events, evoked only emptiness and the desire for emptiness within her. The frame around the patch of wall propelled her on to unpleasant thoughts, so she pulled herself away and inadvertently stumbled onto Tintoretto's grave that was located beneath an inscribed marble slab at her feet.

It was so cold in the church that she imagined she was frozen in a block of ice. Finally, she noticed a painting of the beheading of St. Christopher who, with his naked back to the viewer, was enthralled by the vision of an angel as the executioner behind him was rearing back with his sword to decapitate him. Lilli saw that the angel was floating in a waterfall of light, according to her, and although she admired the painting, she quickly left the building. She could feel how confused she was, and whether she wanted to or not, she had to think about the face and the words of Francesco Galli who had brutally hurt her. But, in retrospect, she understood that she had insulted him first, even though she was only interested in the truth. She now felt satisfaction. "I did it for me!" she said to herself silently. Then she realized that—unintentionally—she must have said it out loud, because a boy on a kick scooter made a large detour around her. She didn't care, she told herself, but she admitted that wasn't true, and that she only was trying to justify the feeling belatedly. "I have to find myself," she concluded.

The canal with the pretty brick homes and bridges gave the impression that she was watching a movie backwards—seen from the end to the beginning. Also, as she walked along the deserted canal, she indulged her impression until the area became more bustling and transformed itself into a well-kept suburb. Tourists and elderly local women pulling shopping carts occupied the street. On the other side of the canal where motorboats were tied up, a large dog with black-and-white spots stared at her. As she stared back at the dog, it became restless, but didn't bark. Most of all she liked the many well-fed cats that slept on the windowsills or watched insects with jerky head movements. She had the impression of being in the true Venice—undisturbed by mass tourism—where people spoke to each other, cooked, watched television, were simply at home. The brick buildings and canals in their stillness even radiated something like "idyll," even if a bit subdued.

Meanwhile she had come to the "Moors Square," the Campo dei Mori whose name, as she knew, came from three large stone sculptures of Oriental figures. They were attached to the walls of a corner house and wore large turbans and splendid caftans. At the corner of the building was the unifying figure, the famous sculpture of the man with the iron nose that represented the satirist Sior Antonio Rioba. In fact, the four figures embodied the three Mastelli brothers and one of their sons. On her travels with Klemens, Lilli had learned that they had originally come from Peloponisia and were erroneously considered Orientals. Back then she had even learned their names, though she had forgotten them in the interim. An ancestor of the brothers had had the iron nose attached to Rioba's stone sculpture because it had become customary to attach long messages to it with mocking verses about the government and the clergy, which had severely damaged the original nose. Lilli had often had lunch or dinner with Klemens in the osteria beside the nose-man, so she didn't hesitate to eat there now. There was only one vacant table, she sat down and ordered a pizza. Since the restaurant didn't carry pizza anymore, she asked for a menu and ordered grilled shrimp on risotto with lemon and chives. But as soon as the waiter had disappeared with her order, she regretted that she hadn't left. On the other hand, she didn't want to return to the Hotel Diana where the ceiling with the strange glass lampshade would fall on her head, so she drank the glass of wine that was in front of her and, when the waiter brought her food, she ordered another.

After she had paid, she quickly stepped out onto the street to see the house, only a few steps away, where Tintoretto had spent the last twenty years of his life. In a niche beside the front door stood the sculpture of the third brother. There was also a marble slab referring to the painter. On the third floor, she noticed green-and-white striped awnings, canopies that were swung out, and from the duplex above, a child was staring at the sky that had grown dark again.

Lilli wanted to keep moving, but she didn't know where. A group of schoolchildren had made up a game or were involved in one that Lilli didn't recognize. They chased each other and attempted to snatch each other's scarves, and whoever succeeded, tried to tie it around his or her neck before the next child took it from them. They played with wild shrieks. Lilli gazed indecisively at her city map, trying to find the closest vaporetto station. To her surprise, it was right nearby, behind the Madonna dell'Orto Church.

On her way, she saw two women standing in an empty alley,

gossiping so enthusiastically that they failed to see that their two dogs were mating. An ardent Pekinese had mounted a white shaggy lapdog that was not much bigger. When the women glanced over at the dogs, they softly screamed, laughed, and pulled the dogs leashes to separate them.

In the waiting platform that was sparsely populated, she could see the Line #41 vaporetto in the distance, approaching under the dark sky, and found the sight—she couldn't explain why—exceptionally beautiful. It was related to a feeling of belonging, she assumed, and also a certainty that she hadn't felt in quite a long time.

The vaporetto was half-empty. It started to rain again, small transparent drops ran down the windows, an industrial crane sailed past, its workers in dark raincoats and hoods. At the next station a nun in white got on, an older woman with a peasant face, wearing a blue vest, black shoes, and carrying a wet black umbrella. She sat down a row ahead of Lilli, sneezed loudly, apologized in a whisper to the old man sitting near her, and kept coughing at regular intervals, until Lilli left the vaporetto at the Sant'Elena station.

She stayed in the waiting platform and, without a second thought, immersed herself in the rain images before her, the sea, pilings that protruded from the water and pointed toward the Lido, passing vaporetti that didn't stop in Sant'Elena. Once again, the sight was beautiful, as if she were seeing everything for the very first time.

She finally boarded the next vaporetto that was also sparsely occupied. The passing Giardini seemed mysterious in the rain, what she saw was overridden by memories—in the end it was the image of Francesco Galli, standing on the shore, looking out at the ocean, saying: "You must hate me, I expect that!" But she didn't hate him, she admitted to herself. She was now upset with herself for her audacity that basically ruled out any further conversation.

It had stopped raining. At St. Marks' Square, two women were pushing cats in small carts that reminded Lilli of kindergarten wagons. The animals meowed pitifully. At first Lilli had only heard the whining behind her, but then she realized the entire calamity. Cat lovers, Lilli knew, were obstinate people . . .

As always, tourists were feeding swarms of pigeons on the Square. A girl was just trying to catch one. She lured the pigeon with bread crumbs and squatted down to the bird . . . Unexpectedly, the girl grabbed for it, but ended up with only feathers in her hand because the bird escaped. The small bunch of feathers was left on the ground, as the girl fled out of embarrassment.

Meanwhile six young policemen—with medals on their chests—strolled St. Mark's in pairs. Also, soldiers in alpine hats mingled with the tourists. Lilli hadn't planned to hang around Caffè Florian, the killing of the policeman and its complications were still too vivid in her mind, but she then resolved to overcome her fears. The usual sounds of the music bands rang out from in front of Caffè Florian and Gran Caffè Quadri.

She later got the idea to more closely observe the photographer in the middle of the Square. The young man stood behind a presumably hundred-year-old camera with its wooden housing on a tripod, though, in reality, it was only a mock-up, as she had known all along. Built inside the box was a Nikon SLR camera, a small parasol protecting it from sun and rain. The people who wanted their pictures taken received bird seed to lure pigeons that then swarmed the people, landing on their outstretched arms, shoulders, and even their heads. When she stood before the young photographer and asked him in English if he had an archive with gazillions of photos, he laughed and replied, to her surprise, also in English: "No, then we'd even have more pictures than the entire Museo Correr!"—She didn't really know why she had spoken to him, she didn't have a reason, and she finally entered Caffè Florian but didn't see the headwaiter Roberto. As she sat down at a table, the band was playing "Amore mio non piangere . . ."

Gulls came flying in, sailed over the heads of the guests, and flew off. They quickly drove off the pigeons. The sky cleared and the clouds drifted away. She could even tell that it was warmer. Individual well-dressed women strolled past—"I'm not alone" she thought—some pulled roller suitcases. Others took their own pictures with cellphones on a selfie stick. From time to time, the bands took a break. She ordered several glasses of spritz and noticed that, at five spots on the Square, puddles of water were spreading from canal manhole covers, giving the impression that *acqua alta* was bubbling up again. At intervals, small waves were forming on the surface of the water as if the water were actually surfacing from down below.

Obese people in all skin colors swarmed the Square, now and then someone passed, carrying a baby. She learned that Roberto, the waiter, had just ended his shift. And more and more people arrived: retirees and conformists, students, mechanics, academics, old mothers and older sons, people with a variety of head coverings, eyeglasses, beards . . . show-offs, introverts, jesters, rejects, mourners in black, the silent and the conversational. The gulls had flown off in the direction of the Basilica, the pigeons, however, had returned to the middle of the Square.

She still didn't want to return to her hotel. The only thing waiting for her there was work, she told herself. She had to read through Klemens' two notebooks about his childhood and youth, but something in her resisted. After she had ordered yet another spritz, she only thought about her encounter with Francesco Galli.

9

Escape to Sant'Erasmo

The next morning, she couldn't remember how she had gotten home. She had dreamed, but no longer knew what. And she didn't want to remember . . . Later on, she went into the bathroom, found the smartphone in her pocket, and saw that in the meantime the police had called six or seven times . . . There were also text messages from Vienna, but she ignored them.

She determined that the calls were from Commissario Luca Zacchini's number. The last calls were from the Commissario's assistant, Perlucci, who, she remembered, had been at the interrogation in her hotel room, along with the translator Gamper. She glanced at the clock, it was 5:52 a.m. . . . She took a pain pill as a precaution, remembered that she had eaten a piece of pastry in the Caffé and felt slightly nauseous. She drank some hot water, laid back down on the bed, and in her confusion dialed the Commissario's number. Half-asleep, he answered with his title and name: "Who's speaking?"

"You called me six times yesterday," Lilli answered in English.

"I've been desperately trying to find you! Where were you?"

Lilli immediately regretted that she had called and realized how foolishly she had acted.

"A fifth policeman was murdered tonight. A staff member at the asilo found him by the Ospedale Umberto I. in Cannaregio, dead

94

with a neck wound . . ." Zacchini spoke broken English.

Shocked, Lilli couldn't speak.

"In just a few days there have been three more police officers killed that we can connect with you," he stammered. "In all cases, you were in the vicinity of the crime scene shortly before or after the killings . . . I eliminate the possibility of coincidence . . . I assume you are in great danger! We've learned that you visited the kindergarten in the former Ospedale yesterday around noon . . . So, by the way you're acting, I assume that you'll want to be taken into protective custody?"

Lilli thought briefly and assumed that the two women in the kindergarten hadn't revealed anything about Francesco Galli.

"Why?" she asked.

"I think you first owe me an answer."

Lilli didn't speak.

"Stay in the hotel until I get there!"

He hung up, again without saying goodbye.

And again, Lilli felt only emptiness inside her . . . but she preferred that to the pain and sorrow. She could easily imagine living with the emptiness. At that moment it even seemed the most obvious choice, and she hoped that this could be her salvation.

When she had showered and dressed, she resolved to take things as they came. She didn't believe that Galli was a serial killer. She assumed that he was a broken man who wanted to reestablish his honor, even if he had acted like the world's biggest asshole to Klemens . . .

An hour later, Zacchini was at her door with Gamper and a policeman, and he entered without a greeting.

He had the policemen wait outside, sat down on a chair, and placed the copy of the black notebook on the table.

"So, what were you looking for at the Ospedale?"

"Francesco Galli," Lilli asserted.

"And did you find him?"

"No."

"What did you do on the grounds?"

"I walked around."

"Why were you looking for Galli in the former Ospedale of all places?"

"Somebody told me . . ."

"Who?"

"It might have been you . . ." Lilli responded in a flash.

"When would I have said that?" Zacchini disregarded her hostile tone.

"When you interrogated me."

"You weren't interrogated, that was just an interview, like now."

"Call it whatever you like—I remember it as an interrogation." She felt that her insecurity had disappeared.

Zacchini also disregarded this remark.

"And what am I supposed to have said?"

"That after his dismissal, Galli was treated for depression in the psychiatric clinic," Lilli said. She was now better able to concentrate. "I don't remember exactly, maybe Alberti told me . . ."

"That's more likely, but he's no longer alive, so we won't be able to ask him if he told you that or not."

"Is it that important?"

"You don't know until later what's important and what's not."

"In any case, I suspected he was in the asilo. I mean, it would have been pure luck if I had really found him . . ."

"You knew in advance that there was an asilo there?"

"No."

"And you thought that the Ospedale was still . . . er . . . running?"

"No."

"Then why did you go there of all places?"

"I guess I was just following my instinct."

"After your visit, a murder was committed there, just like on Pellestrina! And you were the first and only witness to the murder of the policeman at the Bacino!"

Lilli kept listening, and waited.

"Incidentally, it's very odd," Zacchini continued. "All the murder victims were alone and on their way home—even Alberti!"

"Don't you understand that I'm exhausted?" Lilli felt that he was driving her into a corner, and flared up. "Do I have to call a lawyer?"

"I'm sorry, but at the moment you're the only one who can help us . . . You must understand that you yourself are in danger and can't be allowed to investigate on your own."

"I don't care . . ."

"That you're in danger?"

"Yes."

Again, the Commissario disregarded her answer.

"What did Galli say to you when you met him?"

Lilli understood that he had just laid a trap for her.

"Who told you that I met Galli?" she countered.

"I won't reveal that to you at this point."

Lilli was silent.

"There are kindergarten teachers there, Galli has known the principal since his time in the psychiatric ward. Did you speak with her?" Zacchini pressured her.

Lilli knew that the woman in the white smock wouldn't have informed on Galli. Her friendship with him was too close for that. So, she didn't answer.

"You inquired about Galli!" Zacchini insisted.

Lilli could tell that he was skating on thin ice, so she answered in the negative.

"The principal of the kindergarten told us that!"

Lilli felt—though she didn't know why—that she had gained the upper hand.

"The psychiatric clinic is nearby," she responded.

"What do you mean by that?"

"I mean that the patients see reality and their version of reality in the same way."

"So?"

"They don't speak the truth, but try to imagine what might be possible," Lilli explained confidently.

"So, what did Galli tell you?" Zacchini continued resolutely.

"Nothing, because I didn't meet him."

"I've treated you fairly. Actually, I should have taken you down to the station. I can also understand that you want to clear up your husband's death. In that case you should work with us and trust us. If you wish, you can go back to Vienna. If not, then, as I said before, you're in danger."

Lilli didn't budge.

Zacchini also waited.

Several minutes passed. "Okay, fine," Zacchini finally said, but remained seated. After another minute he leaped up, quickly opened the door where the police officer was waiting, let Gamper go first, and closed the door behind him.

Lilli was exhausted. She saw herself lift the telephone receiver, order breakfast brought to her room, and lay down on the bed, fully clothed. She suddenly saw herself in her memories: as she bent down to the murdered police officer and saw the killer running off, as she strolled along the main street of Chioggia, hand in hand with Nicole who distributed gifts, with Galli on the shore behind the Ospedale Umberto I., the gulls screeching under the dark sky, and she also saw her own expression during Commissario Zacchini's interrogation. Nothing seemed preposterous anymore, not even that she had lied, regardless of whether or not it was "normal"— she simply conceded the fact. Lying was part of living, like reality and dreams. She understood that she was now making the same argument for herself as in the interrogation with Zacchini where she had mocked patients in psychiatric therapy by claiming that their concept of reality was the same as actual reality. If she herself was crazy and everybody else was "normal," she told herself, then the world was truly sick, and at the same time knew that it was only half-true.

There was a knock at the door. She got up, opened the door, had the room service waitress put her breakfast tray on the table, and was so clearheaded that she took a five-euro bill from her money purse and gave it to the young woman, all the while seeing herself from a distance—also as she drank tea, spread jam on the white bread, ate, and even when she looked at herself in the mirror. She laid down on the bed again, closed her eyes, and imagined that Galli was speaking with her, seeing his face before her, but not hearing a single word. Of course, she spoke with him, but although she could see herself, she couldn't hear her own words either.

The next time there was a knock at the door and she got up to open it, the phenomenon disappeared in an instant.

"It's too much," she said, unintentionally out loud.

The room service waitress stood in the corridor with her mouth wide open. Was that reality, or was she still dreaming?

She left her room to give staff time to make up the bed, but had no idea where she should go and what she should do. Maybe she could go have a conversation with the skeleton in the pharmacy's display window. The thought stuck in her mind like a chicken bone in the craw. Since she was again thinking about Klemens, she got in the elevator, rode down to the lobby, and as she was about to leave the hotel, the porter spoke to her. He told her that a message had come in, and she accepted the email. She read that the translator, Lanz, on behalf of Egor Blanc, was inviting her to come to the island of Sant'Erasmo. Simultaneously, she could see herself reading the text. At first, she was reluctant to accept the invitation, because she was still trying to deal with Galli's hateful outburst and her accusations. On the other hand, perhaps she could learn something from Blanc about Klemens' death . . .

She requested that the porter confirm the invitation and ask Lanz for details. In addition, she had him send Lanz her email address. Just then she realized she had left her purse in the room and didn't have any money, so she took the elevator back up to the third floor. Once there, she decided to put off reading Klemens' two notebooks with his childhood comics until later.

Suddenly, in the back of her head, she heard Klemens speaking—in the voice that she so missed: "Watch out," he said anxiously, just as she stepped out of the elevator, and she responded out loud: "Yes!" The porter stared at her, startled, but instantly refocused on the piece of paper he had in his hands.

She went over to the desk and requested Lanz's email response.

"It would be best if you came right now. Take the next vaporetto to the Fondamenta Nuove station . . ." she read, and again saw herself reading the message. "From there, take the Line #13 vaporetto to the Sant'Erasmo Capannone station. First you need to get an overview of the island's beauty. Compared to Venice and in the off-season, there are few tourists. After a fifteen-minute walk, you'll come to the Hotel Lato Azzurro where a room has been reserved for you. If you would prefer to be picked up at the vaporetto station, I'll give you the number of the hotel—surprise us! Lanz."

Meanwhile, another email had come in, this one from Michael Aldrian, the magician: "Don't bring anything! We've got everything. As a welcoming gesture, if you arrive before 4 p.m., we'll provide whatever you might need."

"Just a moment!" said the porter. "A gentleman is here to see you. He would like to speak with you."

"What does he look like?"

"Average height, roughly forty years old, and he's wearing a beige summer jacket."

Lilli was convinced that it was probably Police Officer Perlucci who had perhaps been assigned to protect her.

"Well, where is he?"

"He had to go to the pharmacy first . . . something for his wife . . ."

"I have to go to the pharmacy, too . . ."

Lilli took the emails, quickly left the hotel and, without a backward glance, practically ran to the arcades at the Doge's Palace. Once there, she stopped, and when she was certain that she wasn't being followed, strolled along the Grand Canal to the San Zaccaria station. She knew that she had brought along the small mosaic stone. Still, she was aware that she was escaping adversity to find hope, as she told herself.

Unlike Klemens, she had never been on Sant'Erasmo. On his last visit, he had written that he wanted to go back there—this time with her. She liked the thought, because Klemens lived on within her . . . Just the possibility of escaping this Venetian nightmare gave her courage. She wandered along the wharf, avoiding the many souvenir stands with postcards, baseball caps, T-shirts, and scarves, noticing vaporetti, motorboats, and, from a distance, a large ship that was at anchor before the Museo Navale, the naval history museum. Just then, a massive tall ship from the Canale della Giudecca sailed into the Canale di San Marco. She hated the cruise ships and the people, the passengers, who were helping destroy the city—the city that represented all conflicting human qualities like no other city, a brick library where you could discover what human beings are capable of, Lilli thought.

She was just passing by the Hotel Danieli where she had spent a clandestine weekend with Klemens before their marriage.

At the San Zaccaria station, she boarded the vaporetto that would first take her to Sant'Elena.

She noticed a large poster with photographs by Andy Warhol and Robert Rauschenberg—Warhol with a wig and serious, Rauschenberg in a pullover, smiling—as well as an equally large poster displaying a graphic by Mark Tobey: black-and-white, with a touch of blue. It looked like sunlight on small ocean waves.

As the vaporetto docked for the next leg of the journey, she found a vacant window seat that would later offer a good view of the Arsenal's large walls. She had grown accustomed to the sight.

An elderly man—bald, temperamental—and an energetic middle-aged woman came on board, independent of each other. Since there were only two seats left in one row, the window seat was taken and the seat in the middle was the least desirable, an argument ensued. The woman stubbornly insisted on the end seat, even though the man had reached the seat first. The bald fellow argued with her, but in the end, he took the middle seat, shaking his head. His expression was as if his shoes were too tight, and several times he shook his head. A bit later the woman left the end seat and, from the middle aisle, used her flash attachment to photograph the walls around the Arsenal through the closed window. Lilli knew that the woman would later only have captured the reflected flash and a fragment of the outside world on her display. The woman was extremely busy, she suddenly couldn't sit still, couldn't stop taking flash pictures. Lilli noticed that on the ring finger of her right hand she wore a plastic splint that covered back to her wrist. When Lilli saw her face, she was taken aback: a thick beard covered her cheeks, her chin, and even part of her lips.

In the meanwhile, a man that Lilli thought was an approximately 70-year-old homeless person had come on board and taken the woman's seat. His hair was combed back with water. He was wearing a dirty sport coat and avoided looking at people. At first, he had shoved a black duffel bag beneath his seat, but then took it out between his feet, and the next time Lilli glanced over, when she heard a sound, she discovered that he was eating blackberries, smacking his lips and slurping them. He licked and sucked them out of his open hand. He reached into his duffel bag again and hastily devoured another helping. When he had had enough of the blackberries, he simply tossed the rest under the seat in front of him. The man beside him, who had already had an argument with the woman, watched with a disdainful expression, said nothing—even though disgusted—, finally got up, and indignantly went outside to the vaporetto's deck. Meanwhile, the homeless man had taken a paper bag out of the duffel (that featured the inscription "Zucchero" in printed letters), poured granulated sugar into his palm, and began to lick it up. Lilli watched as he repeated this procedure three times, then folded the paper bag and put it back in the duffel, took out another paper bag, held a slice of white bread in his hand, and began to stuff it in his mouth. Lilli thought she could smell alcohol on the man and assumed he was imbibing a hangover breakfast. When he thought no one was watching, he crumpled up the bag and tossed it under his seat so hard that it landed at the feet of a female tourist in a straw sun hat sitting in the row behind him. The woman was gazing out the window and didn't notice.

The man still didn't look at anyone, not Lilli either, who was observing him out of curiosity. She didn't find him obnoxious, and she didn't think he was repulsive: he was chewing the last bit of the white bread so quickly and ferociously, as if he were trying to fend off some impending event.

She noticed that a helicopter was following them.

Now Lilli remembered that she had once seen an old man disembarking at the Rialto Bridge who lost his hat that had fallen to the floor of the vaporetto, and when she called out to him, he hadn't heard her shouting. The vaporetto now had a new hat, Lilli thought.

The was a mob at the Fondamenta Nuove station. At first, she couldn't find the actual waiting platform for the vaporetto to Sant'Erasmo, but when she had finally found it, she couldn't find a vacant seat on the long bench, and discovered from the framed timetable at the entrance and exit that she still had to wait fifty minutes for the next waterbus. All kinds of vaporetti docked, sailed past, just not the Line #13.

Before she could finally board, there was new confusion. Moments ago, a noisy class of schoolgirls had stormed the waiting platform and had lined up in front of the exit, but the girls were waiting for a different ship. They laughed a lot, gestured and discussed, and only reluctantly sat down, while still talking non-stop. In addition, on board she didn't see either the designation for Line #13 or a schedule. Instead, Lilli saw two apparently outdated signs with stations for Line #4.1 on the left- and right-hand side of the sliding door to the passenger cabin. She was in the vaporetto with about ten other passengers and from the front window could see an airliner landing in the distance.

The waterbus first sailed past the San Michele cemetery, then from the extended factories of bare bricks on the island of Murano to the pretty white lighthouse and the church, where they docked.

When the waterbus had resumed its route, a white boat approached, two men in blue-and-white striped shirts—one on each side—at the oars. More often she saw boats with outboard motors, one even had a dog on its prow, seemingly enjoying the trip. As they sailed on, the waterbus came to an area with a low water level and soggy soil where a man in rubber boots was busy collecting clams. He had pulled his motorboat ashore on a bare mud island within sight. For Lilli, he looked incredibly lost.

Tall shrubs bordered the shoreline of the emerging flat island of Vignole. A heron slowly flew off. Glancing down a canal, densely overgrown with bushes, she spotted a wooden bridge in the background. Before that, four motor yachts were moored to poles on the left.

The vaporetto chugged along between the poles, a seagull swam in the water, everything contributed to a feeling of seclusion.

They again stopped at a station, this time at the island of Lazzaretto Nuovo, as Lilli read from a handwritten linen banner above the entrance to a boathouse. She knew that during the plague years up to ten thousand people (who possibly weren't infected) had been quarantined in a huge building complex. In addition, the crew of every ship that came from "oversea" had to spend a three-week incubation period (alongside people who were perhaps infected) before they were allowed to enter the city. There was even a Christian and a Muslim cemetery, and the waterways were clogged with hundreds, even up to a thousand vessels, supply ships and boats with relatives. She got off at the next station.

10

In Paradise

She just started walking. It was so hot that she regretted not having brought a hat. The asphalt street went past a parking lot surrounded by shrubs where countless bicycles and cars were parked, including several three-wheeled Ape mini-trucks. Ahead, a flat landscape with yellow-green blossoming juniper bushes, smaller canals, bridges, fields, cypress trees, and houses with laundry hanging from the windows. She followed the road, crossed a lengthy wooden bridge to the sea and another canal that led to the island's interior. She saw that the houses were far apart, between them were meadows, fields, shrubs, and only isolated groves of trees. The air, driven by wind from the ocean, was marvelously fresh and gently cooled her. She could hear birds chirping the entire time. She paused and now also heard the humming of insects, though they didn't bother her. Along the way, she asked an approaching couple on bikes if it was very far to the "hotel." They slowly shook their heads, and the young man finally replied that it was about another five minutes. A British married couple on foot that she met about fifteen minutes later thought: "around five minutes." But after yet another fifteen minutes, she still didn't see a hotel. When she flagged down an Ape, the driver just pointed in the direction she was going and laughed.

The first pretty bricked "peasant villas"—that's what she called the one-family homes—were neither a hotel nor a restaurant. And there wasn't a soul in the front yards or behind the windows. It took more than half an hour until she saw a wooden house and the ocean in the distance. When she got closer, she saw the Maximilian Tower rising above the shrubbery like a miniature Colosseum: it impressed her as being deserted.

Children were bathing in the dirty water of a concrete harbor basin with motorboats. Beyond that, a bridge and an almost black moat around a fortified tower. She stopped in the midst of birds chirping, heard children shrieking, and looked over at them. Up ahead, a restaurant with an ocean view and a small deserted beach, its sand strewn with trash. Lilli was just about to inquire about the hotel at the restaurant's patio dining area when a man—smoking a cigarette—approached her. "No! No!" he said in garbled English. "Il Lato Azzurro . . ." he pointed in the direction she had just come and shouted *"Destra! Destra!"* Lilli knew that the word "destra" was derived from Latin "dextra" and meant "on the right." She thanked the man and set out. She first came to two lovely country homes with gardens, in one of them swans were pecking in the grass and a motorboat was lying under a fruit tree. She noticed two small sailboats and a rowboat in front of the other building. In the meantime, she had begun to perspire, but the vegetable island that provided the city with its produce, contributed to the fact that she had felt increasingly better ever since her arrival.

Ten minutes later she reached a romantic bridge bordered by small bushes that she had passed earlier without noticing it. She gazed over the railing into a body of water. It was dark-green, overgrown with seaweed, motionless. At some spots she could look right down to the light sandy bottom. A few steps further on, she saw a yellow building, half-hidden by pine and cedar trees. That had to be the hotel, even though she didn't see any signs. The broad entrance stairway with balustrades led up to the second floor. She didn't see a soul.

Finally, an Arabic-looking young woman appeared, holding a key with a room number that she handed to Lilli and then preceded her down the hallway to a door that had the same number as the key. The young woman ran off, and Lilli saw through the room window the canal and the bridge that she had crossed to get to the hotel. To the left was an absurdly tall linden tree that cast its shadow over the square at the front of the building. The low wooden platform and its wooden floor with accompanying tables and chairs were completely shielded from the sun's rays, but she was concerned that there was still no one around.

As she glanced at the bed in her room, she was amazed that three suitcases were lying there, a travel bag on the floor.

There was a knock at the door. It reminded Lilli of the moment when she met Aldrian, the magician, in the Hotel Diana.

Sure enough, he was standing in the corridor and asked if he might come in.

"You'll be wondering why I put the three suitcases and your travel bag in your room. I apologize, but Signor Blanc had notified the Hotel Diana, and I went ahead and settled your bill and collected your luggage. My wife, Beatrice, was with me and, based on the size of your articles of clothing in your suitcase, bought new ones: shoes, a rain cape, an umbrella, a dress, jeans, undergarments, a sport jacket, and toiletries." He smiled. "In the travel bag you'll find the two notebooks in mirror script by Klemens Kuck, the discoverer of fantastic new dimensions and parallel worlds," he concluded, as if he were announcing a magic trick.

Still smiling, he took the third suitcase, opened the lid, and let her look inside, but put his index finger to his lips and whispered: "It's empty. Monsieur Blanc, who invited you, is the greatest magician of all times and in the entire universe. But remember this: Blanc wants to know everything, the smallest bit of trivia. On Blanc's properties, you're never unseen, there are hidden cameras everywhere."

"Here in the hotel, too?" Lilli asked, astonished.

"No. The hotel is clean. He told me to sweep your room when I brought the suitcases."

He reached for the empty suitcase and abruptly ran out the door, without even saying goodbye. Lilli put the other two suitcases beside the travel bag at the foot of the double bed, locked the door behind him, and closed her eyes.

At some point the room phone rang. While reclining, she picked up, but no one was there. This happened again and again, until she leaped up, looked for her deodorant, combed her hair, and left the room.

Along the way, she realized that she had forgotten her wristwatch on the nightstand.

She made a mistake and had not taken the stairs to the terrace, but had found steps down into a workshop. As she crossed the room, she passed by three terrariums with chameleons. An electric motor quietly hummed. She moved closer and observed the animals. Klemens had been crazy about chameleons. He had often said: "Man is descended from chameleons, not from apes." That said: only his brain is chameleon-like, so the change of colors isn't visible.

At an outdoor table sat the translator Lanz with his wife "Caecilia," as he introduced her. Lilli instantly found her to be beautiful and charming.

In the shade of the linden tree, the young Arabian hostess served salad, white bread, salami, prosciutto, cheese, and mineral water, and everything tasted marvelous.

As on her trek to the hotel, Lilli noticed the chirping of birds. She also realized that conversation had come to a halt.

"What do you do here on this sleepy island?" she asked Caecilia.

"For relaxation on the island, I just stare at the sky," the woman replied, and laughed. "No," she continued, "I'm an astronomer at the University of Padua. It just became too demanding to take the vaporetto first thing every morning from Sant'Erasmo to Venice and ride the train to Padua, and then make the entire journey back in the evening . . . It takes much longer than to go from La Giudecca where our house is located."

Lanz nodded, and Lilli asked him—because she already knew that he was a translator—why he was working on Shakespeare and rendering his complete works into Italian.

At that point she realized he was intoxicated.

Lanz smiled. "I had an offer from a publisher and accepted it, that's all . . ." He kept smiling and spoke slowly. "I had become fascinated by Shakespeare while I was still at the university . . . I took every opportunity to get a ticket for any premieres at the Burgtheater . . . It was then that I got to see the actual plays . . . I discovered that they are like self-analyses of the author and—this is the unique part—also analyses of humanity . . . absolutely . . ." He sank back into his thoughts, suddenly laughed, and called out: "Absolutely! That word could come from Shakespeare . . . I mean, it's the expression of a result, based on the word 'absolute' . . ." He laughed once again. "We are convinced that we understand other people, but that's a mistake. We don't even understand ourselves, even though we believe that we know everything about ourselves. Our next mistake! It's just the opposite—we are at the mercy of our egos."

He amused Lilli, so she egged him on. "And Shakespeare . . . how was he able to know so much about everything?"

Lanz was saying that Shakespeare had uncovered the disparity between peoples' thoughts and deeds, which made Lilli suddenly take notice. She had been struggling with this problem since childhood.

"You can understand people only through this contradiction, which no one wants to acknowledge," Lanz continued. "It originates in the urge to gain dominance and to avoid perishing. Shakespeare was a visionary, blessed with a marvelous gift for language with which he could transform the most improbable things into reality," he raved. "The interior and exterior lives of his figures are in constant interaction. They kill, they hope, they hate and fall in love, and, on top of that, they behave like members of cults . . . once they have embraced an ideology, a conviction . . ."

"I understand that . . ." Lilli interrupted. But before she could join in, the translator continued his rant: "Ideologies constantly provide brainwashing until a person becomes silent and is nothing but a programmed figure in a computer game that someone else is playing . . . You can find this realization throughout Shakespeare's works. It's like an entomologist's microscope that enormously magnifies the insect's eyes and legs and mouth and antennae and shows them in the minutest detail . . . Each person has just *one* skill at his or her disposal," he continued excitedly, "the skill of lying and the magic tricks of intrigue and denunciation." He burst out laughing. "They belong to mankind, like breathing in and breathing out. Incidentally, there is a correlation to this aptitude in the animal kingdom: camouflage, mimicry, ambush. You can find it everywhere—on land, in the water, in the air." He paused again. "If you follow the explanations of various religions that peace prevailed in Paradise, then plants and animals must also have been cast out of Paradise, perhaps because of the pomegranate and the snake," he went on, and again burst out laughing— "because they are mortal like us and have learned to deceive. Back then, Paradise was dissolved. It was suddenly gone, everyone and everything was cast out." He fell silent, before changing the topic. "I'm leaving the island in the next couple of days. Not just to make my wife's life easier, but also because something like a cult has grown up here on Sant'Erasmo. All organizations, even those that have an ideology of doing good, continue to evolve according to the law that Shakespeare formulated in his works."

"Come!" Caecilia said to Lilli and got up. "Let me show you the garden. It's paradisiacal, in spite of everything that's been said."

They walked around the hotel that was much larger than she had originally thought. Several times she spotted lizards that were sunning or seemed to be sleeping, but as soon as she got close, they scampered away. Yard-long columns of hundreds of snails in their shells clung to the walls of the building where a window ledge protruded or two walls formed small niches. Lilli also noticed snail columns on the branches of trees.

"The snail shells—according to Signor Blanc—represent the past," Caecilia began. "And the lizards, with their quiet waiting or rapid vanishing, the present. But the birds that you hear on all sides represent the future."

"What about Signor Blanc?" Lilli asked. "Is he the cult leader that your husband was talking about?"

"Signor Blanc," Caecilia responded in a low voice, "to whom we owe a lot, if not everything, is a very old man . . . He suffers from memory loss . . . Earlier, he could retain everything in his mind . . . He now demands that every event be recorded on computer, and since he's been living on Sant'Erasmo, he has the entire area under guard. He mistrusts his half-brother more than anyone else."

"Why is that?"

"He doesn't want to bequeath him anything, because he doesn't trust him . . . But Signor Blanc continually irritates his colleagues, some of them had become paranoid and fled the island. I think he considers himself to be someone from whom you can't hide anything. On the other hand, he is overflowing with kindness."

"Why did he invite me?"

"I assume that he regrets your husband's death and wants to make you happy."

Together, they made their way back to their table and found that Lanz had fallen asleep. Caecilia lovingly woke him and asked him to follow her to the car.

"Be seeing you," Lanz called as he left.

Alone, she circled the hotel once more, because she also wanted to see the fourth side of the building. To her surprise, she found pine and fig trees, laurel bushes, and behind them, grey in the sunlight, flat fields as far as the eye could see, interspersed with more pines. Butterflies fluttered over the meadows and shrubbery.

Farther ahead, two large tents had been set up. She could hear the muted sounds of a chainsaw, and when Lilli came closer, she saw that two Africans were working in an improvised workshop. Bicycles were parked in the other tent.

She sat down again under the linden tree. Now and then she could hear hammering and snippets of conversation coming from the bicycle workshop, a small white dog busily ran in and out.

At some point, a man in a red polo shirt, gold-rimmed glasses, and a blue squashed sun hat came out of the hotel. His hat was exceptionally tall, she estimated about eight inches and assumed that the older gentleman was bald . . . His wife, her hair dyed brown, followed him sullenly. They soon began to quarrel in muffled voices, looked around and, with their backs to Lilli, walked toward the fields where they apparently exchanged angry gestures.

"Reality," Lilli thought, "is basically more complicated than any science and any religion. No one really knows their way around. Everything is always an attempt at an explanation." She had always considered the two halves of her brain as labyrinths where thoughts strayed, and she felt as if she had been born into this maze of reality that no one understood . . . She realized that she couldn't infer the entire St. Mark's Basilica from one little mosaic stone. But she could never grasp the "entire picture" anyway. She was just a tiny insect that had found its way into a mighty building. If you solved one puzzle, another one took its place. Reality seemed to her like a many-headed Hydra. If you cut off one of the mythological figure's heads, two new ones popped up.

After a while, the old couple returned—the woman several yards ahead of the man who followed grumpily, his head down. It was obvious that the woman was insulted. The man glanced up as they passed by the tent with the bicycle workshop, observed the two Africans with little interest, and acted as if it had nothing to do with him. He unlocked the mini-bus with the hotel's logo that was parked under the tall linden tree, got in, and looked back at his wife, who had apparently forgotten something. He then adjusted the rearview mirror so that he could see the hotel better without having to turn his head, leaned back, and now had a newspaper in his hands that he unfolded.

Lilli suddenly had a desire to return to Venice. She ran to her hotel room, took her watch from the nightstand, grabbed her two suitcases, shouldered her travel bag, and flew down the stone stairway to the garden. The woman had just gotten into the bus with her husband, had thrown the newspaper out of the rolled-down window, and hissed something nasty at him as the man with the too-tall sun hat stared through the windshield at the trunk of the giant linden tree. His wife was silent, head lowered. Suitcases in hand, Lilli called out that he should stop, but the driver was apparently so preoccupied with their argument—maybe he didn't even want to take notice of her—that he stepped on the gas. So, Lilli dropped her luggage onto the wooden platform and cussed to relieve the pressure. Since she was now standing right beside the discarded newspaper, she bent down and saw five photos on the front page that apparently depicted the murdered police officers. She sat back down at the table and opened the paper, but she couldn't understand the article since it was written in Italian. She could only deduce that it was an extended article about the police murders in Venice.

Since she didn't want to go back up to her room, her luggage was left standing on the platform. She noticed that a brown-and-green spotted lizard was sunning itself at the next table and couldn't be disturbed. Lilli loved the pattern of light and shadows underneath the linden tree. What was she waiting for now? She could simply take a bicycle and forget her luggage. Besides, she had to go to the bathroom, so she hurried to the stone staircase where she encountered the next lizard that she unintentionally scared off by her dash.

On her way back, she noticed more lizards between the building and the stone staircase, and a lone one lying on the balustrade. Presumably they even got into the empty rooms. Since it was quiet—except for the noise from the workshop that they were obviously accustomed to—the little reptiles were now crawling out all over the place. One was even clinging to the wall beside the main entrance, like the snail columns in the wall niches.

Lilli's glanced at the tall fig bushes. A mechanic began hammering again, she gazed over at him for a moment, and when she looked back at the door, the lizard had disappeared. The small white dog that she had first noticed in front of the tent with the workshop, was now searching under the tables for a treat that someone might have dropped. It found one, looked up, and ran off. Its large ears flopped about, like two cabbage butterflies. In the meantime, one of the Africans was intensely working on an old metal garden table.

Lilli was bored.

She had the impression that the birds were now chirping louder . . . And she was still bored . . . Besides the sound of the chainsaw from the tent, she could now also hear the noise of a compressor, followed by apparently compressed air hissing and puffing over a wooden board.

To her surprise, a short nervous woman in an airy summer frock with high-healed sandals suddenly came down the stone steps, ignored Lilli's presence, looked for an ashtray, sat down in the sunshine, smoked and, without looking up, busied herself with her smartphone. Lilli was relieved. She noticed that the woman's finger- and toe nails were polished. Impatient, she finished her activity, put on glasses, and was about to head back to the stone steps. At that moment Lilli was finally able to free herself from the paralysis that the boredom had caused. She also stood up and called to the woman in English, asking if she knew when the next vaporetto was expected.

The woman turned, smiled, and posed the counter-question as to how she was hoping to get her luggage to the station? Lilli hesitated answering. The woman had an amused expression and explained that she, too, had to get back to Venice.

But where's the car? Lilli asked herself. The chirping of the birds got even louder, butterflies floated past, and one of the mechanics was just changing the inner tube on a bicycle tire.

The woman came back, got a car key from one of the Africans, helped Lilli load her suitcases on the bed of the Ape, put her travel bag there, too, and explained that Lilli would have to sit on a suitcase. The woman then got behind the steering wheel of the one-seater. They crossed the bridge and chugged merrily along to the vaporetto station. Once there, the stranger went to a nearby farmhouse, handed off the key to a woman who lived there, asked Lilli to wait for her, and introduced herself: her name was Dr. Falchi, she was a lawyer who worked for Signor Blanc, she said, and seemed to know a lot about him. Just then Lilli remembered that the newspaper was still in her handbag, and as she was discarding it in a trashcan, the lawyer mentioned that the police were on the trail of a suspect.

Behind them, ducks quacked in the meadow, a swan among them, Lilli noted. The lawyer was busy on her smartphone again, raised her head and explained they had missed the vaporetto and that the next one wouldn't dock for another 35 minutes. She sighed, put the phone in her handbag, and stood beside Lilli who continued to gaze at the ducks.

"I know who you are," the lawyer said after a pause. "I knew your husband, Klemens. We were introduced in Caffé Florian, and he asked me all about Commissario Francesco Galli who supposedly was his father. I know that you were the first person on the scene following the murder at the Bacino. You must have seen at least the silhouette of the killer . . . I know about the events surrounding Guido Alberti in Chioggia, and there are indications that you are suspected of having met Galli in the Ospedale Umberto I."

Lilli avoided looking the lawyer in the eye. Instead, she asked herself where all this was heading. What did she want from Lilli?

She took several steps toward the meadow and didn't look back, but she could hear that Dr. Falchi was following. There was humming birdsong as they walked beneath two old fruit trees, the meadow was entirely covered in white clover.

"I know that Signor Blanc invited you," the lawyer began again. "He wanted to offer you refuge and tranquility in the hotel. But perhaps something there bothered you . . . You had contact with Aldrian, with Lanz and his wife. Lanz is going back to his house on La Giudecca to continue his Shakespeare translation. Perhaps the two of them told you something that now makes you want to get off the island?"

Lilli just shook her head. Three ducks had nestled under the smaller fruit tree, the others had started searching for food in a cornfield.

Lilli turned back and, without speaking or looking around, went down the stone steps beside the low wall to the waiting platform. At first, she sat there, alone. She saw nearby young rowers, standing in boats, as they trained to be gondoliers amid much laughter. Now and then, boatloads of tourists droned past. They gawked at the landscape, seemingly thinking about something else entirely. The waiting platform rocked, creaking and groaning in the choppy water. The sounds, Lilli felt, resembled the noise from closet doors that hadn't been used in a long time. She had consciously ignored what the lawyer had told her. At that moment Dr. Falchi entered the waiting platform.

"Please don't misunderstand me. I want to offer you my assistance. Before you have any further conversations with Commissario Zacchini, please give me a call. I'll give you my private number. Don't worry, Signor Blanc will cover all expenses."

"Why?"

"He says he knows your husband's work and couldn't allow you to suffer further anguish."

Lilli hesitantly accepted the woman's business card, put it in her purse without reading it, and could now see in the distance a blue vaporetto approaching, though it was much smaller than the others.

"We can also go back to the hotel on Sant'Erasmo. I guarantee that you will be left alone."

Lilli shook her head.

"Perhaps you would at least want to stay in Venice?"

Lilli remained silent.

"I can offer you a hotel that you'll like. In any event, Signor Blanc would like you to be his guest."

"I don't understand you and I don't know him . . . Why do I suddenly play a part in his considerations?" Lilli responded impatiently.

Dr. Falchi just shrugged her shoulders without comment.

At that point Dr. Falchi remarked in an offended tone that she simply wanted to offer her assistance . . .

11
Adrift

The following morning, as Lilli looked out the fifth-floor window of the Pensione Wildner, she was practically spellbound. Before her, the panorama of the city: the island of San Giorgio Maggiore with its tall church tower, the equestrian statue of Victor Emmanuel II., the Santa Maria della Salute at the end of the Grand Canal, but especially St. Mark's Bay, the ocean, and the sky. Vaporetti and gondolas moved like toys on the water. The Riva degli Schiavoni below her was already full of tourists, but from up here in the "crow's nest," as she called it, she could only hear muffled sounds.'

After a breakfast in the winter garden that left her with the impression that she was in a 3D movie, she briefly considered what she might do that day. A waiter then approached discreetly and handed her a folded page with a printed email message. It was from Guido Alberti's wife, Lisa, who asked her to take the Line #20 vaporetto at 3:10 p.m. to the island of San Lazzaro where Lisa would be waiting. The return trip would have to be at 5:20 p.m. with the same line, since you can only arrive and leave the Armenian Monastery at those times.

Lilli wondered how Lisa knew that she was staying at the Pensione Wildner. She tried to reach Lisa on the phone, but no one answered.

The hotel had Wi-Fi, and Lilli got her iPad from the room to find out more about the island, because Klemens had been there twice during his last visit. She wondered who he had been looking for? San Lazzaro, she read, had originally been a shelter for lepers . . . then, two hundred years ago, Armenian monks settled the island. The monastery had a library of some 200,000 books and a large collection of Oriental and Armenian manuscripts, as well as an Egyptian mummy. In addition, the English poet, Lord Byron, had lived in the monastery to learn Armenian. She had already been aware of that fact from stories Klemens had told her.

Lilli deliberated for a moment, then decided to first visit the Guggenheim Museum so that she would have more time to think.

She took the vaporetto to Accademia, strolled down a narrow alley and over a stone bridge to reach the building with its modern art. On the way, she began to perspire and have circulatory issues . . . A poster by Mark Tobey in the vaporetto platform on Sant'Elena had reminded her of the Guggenheim Museum. She now wanted to return to the pension, but she forced herself to keep moving forward, to reach her destination. Fortunately, no one was standing in line at the ticket counter.

She sat down in a small stone pavilion in the garden near Peggy Guggenheim's burial urn and the ashes of her fourteen lapdogs that she had called her "babies."

She caught her breath on the shady bench and recalled one of her visits with Klemens . . . She suddenly lost her train of thought, the film broke, and she was in a darkened movie theater . . . Which cinema? Afraid of losing consciousness (that she had just lost), she stood up. She briefly thought she could feel the earth rotating, but then nothing else.

The first thing she saw was the face of an Asian woman, bending over her like a mother over her child's baby carriage. Her attendant helped Lilli up so she could sit on the pavilion's stone bench. Lilli first thought that the "Chinese woman" was touching in her concern, but then she disappeared. I just have to wait, Lilli thought. A gentle breeze wafted from time to time, and each time, as it momentarily got cooler, she felt better. But she didn't want to leave the museum grounds without having taken a look at the Mark Tobey exhibition. She knew she could be headstrong and stubborn. And she counted on that fact. She didn't spend much time there, and after she had exited the building, she sat down, exhausted, on a chair beneath the glass roof at the café entrance. She only glanced up fleetingly, because it made her dizzy, but in her head Mark Tobey's pictures were intermingled with foliage from the previous year still lying on the glass roof and with the thick fresh-green leave of the trees high above. The vision expressed her thoughts and feelings. Tobey's works primarily consisted of mark-, line-, and plant-fragments. And she now had the impression that, first and foremost, he had invented his own script that went beyond formulas and scintigrams—something like a Morse code of his impressions.

When Lilli was confronted with artworks that moved her, linguistic formulations originated in her brain almost automatically, attempted translations from picture into speech.

Once again, she stared up at the glass roof. She now unexpectedly felt such a strong longing for her inner world that she would have loved to remain seated under this glass roof and continue pursuing her thoughts. So, she took her smartphone out of her pocket and—leaning back in her chair—began to photograph everything that was lying on the glass roof. The first picture looked like an illustration for the concept of "epiphany": the sunlight broke through the new green leaves on a branch and onto the old dead foliage, giving her the impression that she was on the bottom of a lake, overgrown with plants, and looking up at the sky. The impression was intensified in the shady areas. What surprised her was the condition that the imaginary water also reflected the light to some degree beneath its surface, as if half-melted sheets of ice were turning and rotating on their axis. Some of the young leaves were so penetrated by the sunlight that they assumed a light-pink color amid the green and the black foliage. The impressions led her to dream: at one point, it seemed as if green water was inhabited by turtles whose shells were facing her; then again, countless birds overhead cast black shadows onto the branches of a broadleaf tree. She was especially

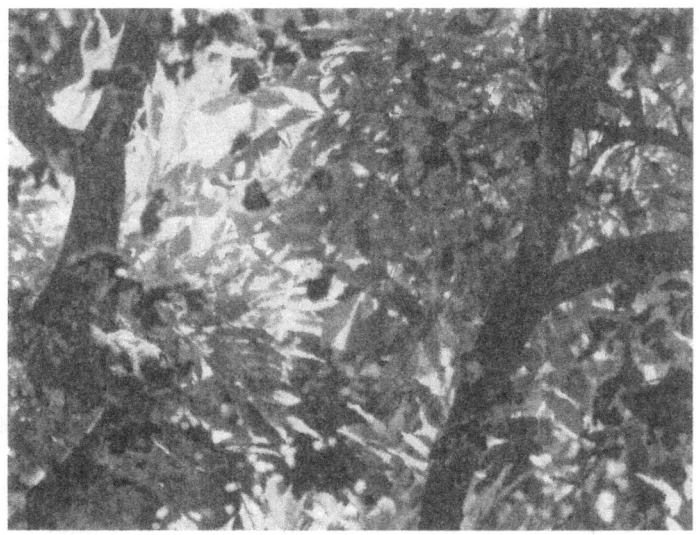

impressed by the surreal concept that the ocean's surface was a transparent mirror, on the upper surface as well as on the underside, that reflected everything above, as well as what was happening in its depths. If the mirror broke, then the shards reflected the various perspectives, since the images were frozen inside them. The picture changed from the Cubist to the Surreal and back again. That reminded her of the broken windowpanes in René Magritte's painting *The Domain of Arnheim*. At the spot on the glass roof where a great deal of dead foliage had collected, she saw an army of bugs and large insects that reminded her of science-fiction movies or of red-and-black monarch butterflies that wintered on a few acres in the Mexican Sierra Nevadas, and when they left in spring, formed clouds of several hundreds of millions of butterflies.

Her brain kept working, though she had quit photographing some time ago and was now approaching the exit without so much as having glanced at the museum's other artworks that she loved so much. She was sorry, but she was too tired and worried that she might miss the vaporetto to Lazzaro degli Armeni. Her focus was still on her inner world, so she only registered her surroundings in bits and pieces—especially the other passengers in the vaporetto—

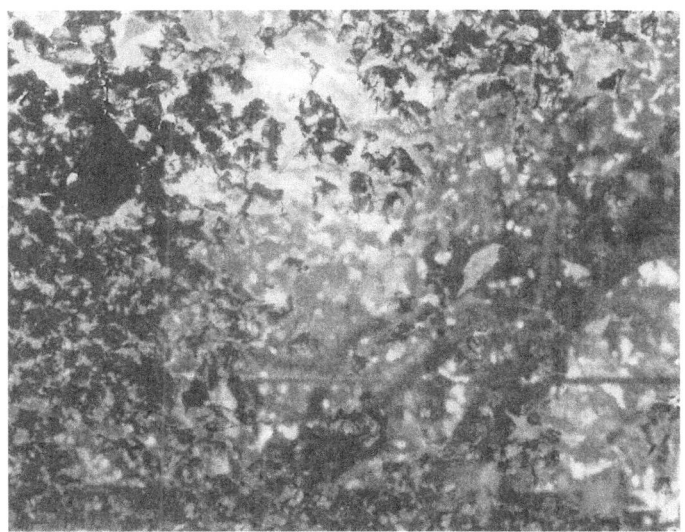

as if they were "dead foliage."

Back in the Pensione Wildner, she had room service bring 'a little something" up to her room, slept for an hour, then woke up just in time to catch the vaporetto. No one had called her in the meantime. And even her most recent attempts to reach Lisa Alberti had been unsuccessful.

The small waiting platform at the San Zaccaria station slowly filled up. She knew that San Lazzaro lay beyond San Servolo, the island with the former "Insane Asylum." Klemens had always been drawn to the place. He used to say that it wasn't the insane who waged wars and killed people, but the sick normal folks who always wanted to be the benchmark in every society.

The closer the small vaporetto came to the former asylum, the more she imagined herself—without really wishing it—playing the part of a sick person who had to say goodbye to the city and was brought to this island that was reserved for insanity. But the only people there were sick in body and soul, along with "normal" doctors and caregivers. To add to their mental breakdown, they also suffered isolation.

When she turned around, the teeny-tiny Campanile and the

Doge's Palace greeted her from afar.

How had the patients on San Servolo passed the time? she wondered. They could probably take the same walk in the same park every damn day, take up hobbies or garden, and wait for visitors.

Everyone but Lilli got off the small vaporetto, presumably to visit the museum at the former asylum. She noticed that the white buildings had numerous windows that seemed to her like bad omens. She considered that medicine in those days was groping in the dark when it came to treatment of the mentally ill, that the disadvantaged were exposed to senseless tortures, and she understood that anyone who was sent here and wasn't already "insane," would have inevitably become so.

She was again irritated that Lisa Alberti had asked her to come to the monastery on San Lazzaro. Why had she arranged everything so secretively?

Meanwhile, the island was now in sight. A rust-red monastery, a church tower, a park.

A bald, bearded man was standing on the jetty at the station. She got off, and the vaporetto sailed away. When Lilli spoke to the stranger in English, he rudely brushed her off and, with gestures and shouting, indignantly made it clear to her that he felt he wasn't responsible for her, and with great exaggeration, finally pointed her to the scenic plateau in the small park.

Steps led upwards, and on the way, Lilli thought that Lisa would be waiting for her, but there was no one in sight. She sat down at a table and gazed at the sea or at the island of San Servolo, at the Campanile and the Doge's Palace that appeared like toy models on the horizon.

As she walked to the main building, she saw a sign on one of the rust-colored walls that told her what she already knew: that Lord Byron, who died at a young age in the Greek War of Independence, had studied the Armenian language on his many visits to the monastery. The water around the island shimmered in the sunlight; above her, "the seemingly boundless blue dome of heaven's air," Lilli thought. She now recalled that it was noticeably cooler on the island than in the city. More than anything else, she could feel a breeze.

At that moment, a monk, dressed in black, addressed her and asked if she was Frau Dr. Kuck? He led her to the front entrance that was embellished in wrought iron.

Lilli kept wondering what Lisa Alberti wanted from her? She couldn't think of any reason why they would have to meet in the monastery on the island. Could it be a trap?

Just then she noticed that a school class was visiting, their backpacks lying on a long bench along one wall, and soon a chatty group of young boys and girls appeared, disciplined and orderly, and left the building with their teacher.

Meanwhile, another monk had silently led her into the monastery garden that was surrounded by arcade walkways. Plastic bags were covering the palms and olive trees. Are they still there from the winter? As protection from some sort of tree disease? she wondered. The monk's gestures gave her to understand that he was deaf, and, smiling in a childlike manner, encouraged her to walk the rest of the way alone. Now Lilli assumed that she was about to meet Lisa or some stranger. She took her time. When she turned around, the deaf monk had disappeared.

The shrubs in the garden had been neatly trimmed and cautiously revealed white and yellow blossoms. The first flowers were emerging from the tilled beds. Shadows delicately tinged the arches of the white cloister on the opposite wall. Without hurrying, she inspected the plants between the arcade arches: roses, iris, begonias, sage, geraniums, and clubmoss. Archeological discoveries were displayed along the walls of the cloister: a gravestone, a baptismal font, a headless statue "from Aquileia." In the adjoining church she noticed three windows behind the main altar that had exquisite stained glass. The window on the right, as she had read in the Internet, portrayed the famous Saint Mashtots, the inventor of the Armenian alphabet. She was excited that the inventor of an alphabet was a saint and that now he was worshipped as a statue in the church.

There were four columns to the left and right of the altar, connected by pointed arches, everything richly embellished with mosaics and ornamentation. Above, the blue-painted heaven with golden stars. In fact, the church was a con-glomeration of various style elements, with Gothic pointed arches, but elsewhere something of a mosque or a Sephardic synagogue. Of course, its walls and side altars were generously decorated with paintings. Lilli glanced around, but no one had followed her, so she went on to the refectory, the monastery's dining hall, a room with head-high wood paneling and white walls above that.

Why had Lisa Alberti chosen this spot for a meeting? Perhaps because it promised security . . . It possibly had to do with Klemens' death . . . and possibly someone had trusted a monk. If that were the case, then why? People could possibly call Klemens an agnostic, but in this regard, he had always been good for a surprise, as Lilli remembered.

As she walked on, she saw a thirty-yard-long walkway with framed pictures—the "Gallery"—even though she wasn't interested in any of the paintings. Other rooms displayed a collection of "European painters," eliciting the same reaction. Her interest was aroused only when she came to the library, because it extended over several rooms.

Suddenly she saw . . . Klemens . . . ahead of her. He was standing motionless between the bookshelves and had a serious expression as he faced Lilli. It lasted just a second before the lights went out in the windowless room. Before her eyes could adapt to the darkness, it became light again. She wasn't surprised that Klemens had disappeared again, his appearance had been the surprise. She was convinced that she had really seen him. The deaf monk suddenly appeared between the bookshelves and excitedly motioned for her to move on, in the same direction where Klemens must have fled. Now Lilli didn't want to lose any time.

The monk huffed and puffed behind her. She stopped and waited to let him pass, but he, too, stopped and waited until he had enough air in his lungs, and instantly transformed himself back into a frantic moron who didn't understand what had just transpired, but did want her to leave the monastery.

Meanwhile she had reached the "Lord Byron Room." But she quickly realized that it was actually a space for Egyptian art, except for the portrait of the English poet that hung over the entrance. Under a glass showcase was a black mummy, covered with a richly-decorated blue wrapping. Just then the deaf-mute monk stormed back in. With gestures and loud grunts, he urged her to rush on, and she fled through a collection of elaborately and colorfully designed Armenian porcelain. The corridor led her into a small treasure room. What little she could later remember were individual books bound in silver, choir surplices, paraments, gold crowns for Mass, chalices, urns, and vials.

The monk caught up with her again in the more-recently-built, modern-looking circular building. He was still trying to catch his breath. Lilli was surrounded by manuscripts—treatises on Scriptures, rituals, sermons, historic texts (as she knew), as well as hymns, but also medical documents, law books and songbooks, breviaries, biographies, and the legends of saints. Many of the originals on display in the cases were lavishly illustrated—the remainder were arrayed on bookshelves from the floor to the ceiling. She had learned from the Internet that a few were more than a thousand years old.

As she left the monastery, the deaf monk ignored her. He hadn't looked her in the eye the entire time, and had treated her as if she were insignificant.

Seated on the hill with the scenic plateau, she was still confused and couldn't think straight. What did Lisa Alberti have to do with all this? Lilli didn't believe in occult phenomena or that she had lost her mind. In fact, the behavior of the deaf monk had seemed crazy from the start, and he hadn't been up to the occasion. Actually, she should be even more upset or unhappy than she really was, but she was just aggravated, and felt as if she had been led around by her nose. She kept thinking that the monk must have been involved in the encounter for which she could find no rational explanation.

She dialed Zacchini's number and told him that she was outside the Lazzaro degli Armeni monastery and didn't know where to go now . . . The Commissario was in a bad mood, responded only with "yes" and "wait," and hung up.

All of a sudden, a voice spoke to her in English. She turned, and was amazed to see Francesco Galli.

"It wasn't my intention to flee. The monk panicked and turned off the light. I'm sorry," he said.

Lilli noticed that Galli was wearing the same clothes as in the Ospedale Umberto I.

"He was probably afraid that the abbot might come with some visitors." He gave a short laugh.

"I've known the monks for many years," he went on. He paused for a long while. "In the meantime, a sixth policeman has been murdered. He was found in the Pierluigi Penzo soccer stadium on Sant'Elena. He had been stabbed elsewhere and then brought there afterwards. Go into hiding, as soon as possible. Best you do it today, but after 10 p.m. when the city is deserted. Leave your luggage in the hotel, you'll get it back. Don't tell anyone about your plans, and don't tell them that you met me . . . I saw Klemens in Venice and he forgave me."

In the next instant, Galli ran down the steps from the scenic platform and disappeared in the darkness.

12

The World in Her Head

She had taken the vaporetto for the return trip and, once onboard, informed Zacchini of that fact. To her surprise, Francesco Galli was not onboard. The waterbus chugged in the direction of St. Mark's Square. She thought that in case Zacchini was waiting for her, she had to be careful not to say anything contradictory or self-incriminating, and on the other hand, pacify him with half-truths.

Fortunately, the Commissario hadn't come to the Pensione Wildner himself, and his assistant, Perlucci, only spoke limited English. So, he spoke broken English with her in the lobby. She told him that her dead husband had often visited the island of San Lazzaro, and she learned from his Venice notes that on this final visit he had been to the monastery two or three different times. That didn't surprise her, she emphasized, because her husband had often thought about religion.

Perlucci wanted to know if she knew who he had been looking for or had met.

Lilli just shook her head.

Why hadn't she informed the police about her intention to go to the island?

At this point Lilli had to ask herself why she wasn't sharing all she knew, and, without much thought, found the answer: she didn't trust Commissario Zacchini . . . . From the outset he had been convinced that Francesco Galli was the culprit, or at least the prime suspect. He would probably reject the thought that Egon Blanc could be behind everything—at least he didn't seem to have seriously considered this possibility. That was understandable in light of Blanc's generous donations and philanthropy, and she secretly was upset that Galli so vehemently blamed the billionaire—but gradually she, too, began to suspect the wealthy stranger.

As Perlucci continued to ask more and more questions, she wanted him to tell her what he himself thought. Perlucci scratched his head and gazed out the lobby window. Lilli repeated the question, but Perlucci just stared out toward the ocean and shrugged his shoulders.

Today, at the soccer stadium on Sant'Elena, a sixth murdered policeman had been found, he finally answered, probably to evade her question. He then pulled himself together and concluded that the police would find the killer who had made mistakes, and these would lead the police to the people responsible for the murder. But it was too early to say for sure.

"Galli and who else?" Lilli asked, warily.

"No. Not Galli." They expected that organized crime was involved . . .

He took out his smartphone and called the Commissario. After a back-and-forth, he announced to Lilli that Zacchini would meet her in the Pensione Wildner the following day. "Tomorrow. He asks that you not leave the hotel in the meantime, or that you at least inform him in case you have an urgent errand . . ." He thought for a second, then added: "If you want to speak with the woman lawyer or see a doctor . . ."

How did he know that she had spoken with a woman lawyer on Sant'Erasmo?

Perlucci left a short time later. If he had only stayed for another 30 seconds or so, he would have found out that Lilli received yet another message—this time from an anonymous writer—in capital letters on a slip of paper and in an empty envelope: "In front of the Museo Ca'Rezzonico, tomorrow at 2 p.m."

"Who left this message?" Lilli asked the porter.

"It was lying on the desk—I was busy with guests who had just arrived."

It was clear to Lilli that the writer must have known Klemens very well, because her husband had loved Ca'Rezzonico in particular. She, however, would have preferred the Museo Querini Stampalia to the Ca'Rezzonico, since she loved Carlo Scarpa's garden and, in the museum, Giovanni Bellini's painting of *The Presentation of Jesus in the Temple*.

In her room in the Pensione, she recalled that Klemens had closely examined Bellini's painting in the Querini Stampalia Museum each time, but had then hurried on to the pictures by the "creators" of comic-book art, Pietro Longhi and Gabriele Bella. And each time there was just a hint of sarcasm that she felt related either to her as an art historian or to the "art world" that (in his opinion) didn't fully appreciate Longhi and Bella. At first, she had also been skeptical, because their skill at painting "hadn't exactly bowled her over." But then she discovered what had aroused Klemens' enthusiasm: the "speaking pictures," as he argued. The presentation was what made it a predecessor of comic-book art. The events were comprehensible only when you read gestures, facial expressions, personal behavior, and expressive clothing. Longhi loved painting pictures depicting the private sphere. Klemens had also called Longhi's paintings "colored pictures as slow-motion silent film" or compared them with the moment when a photographer at the end of the 19th century with his plate camera encouraged his subjects to hold still for five seconds. Bella, on the other hand, painted mass gatherings, his pictures presented an ant colony: festivals, games, Mardi Gras, ceremonies, folk customs—the individual was lost in the crowd.

As the years went by, the Museo Querini Stampalia changed radically. It was rebuilt in one fell swoop, and each time they visited, "something new had been renewed" in the interim, as Klemens had jokingly said.

Fifteen year earlier—on their first visit to the Querini Stampalia

Museum—photographing had not been allowed. In the meantime—since the invention of the smartphone with camera—they had given up trying to monitor everything. In February of 2006, Klemens had been able to photograph—still without permission—pictures on display. First the Scarpa architecture in the corridors, then individual paintings, finally the garden . . . During his winter walk he had been warned not to take pictures by the incensed woman in charge of the store. She had put on her coat specifically to run out into the cold and confront him. When Klemens was on his way out, she once again warned him; he dryly replied that he didn't accept the camera ban, photographing outdoors was permitted everywhere. And, besides, there were no signs in the garden prohibiting it. Another time—it could have been before or slightly thereafter—she recalled that at the entrance to the third floor they had heard chamber music by Vivaldi, followed by sustained applause from an audience. They went into the hall, but the concert had just ended and they only got to see the musicians with their original instruments from the time of the Baroque. The Ca'Rezzonico had the better paintings, as far as she was concerned, but no Bellini.

At some point Lilli must have fallen asleep on her bed in the Pensione, because when she awoke—it was already night outside—she realized that she still had her shoes on and hadn't taken off her dress. She didn't want to look at the clock. To forget time was a small adventure that she had acquired in childhood when she had awoken during the night.

She had been born in Hamburg. Her father came from an affluent family of lawyers and had been a prominent attorney in the city. Her mother taught geography and history at a high school. Lilli lived in their villa on the bank of the Alster with her parents, a younger sister, Isabella, and an older one, Gabriele. She spent her childhood (which she fondly recalled) in the garden on a meadow beneath trees and on the water. There were sailing tours with her father, conversations with her mother and two sisters along with a black Lab "Goofy"—named after the Walt Disney dog with the black floppy ears, the loopy friend of Mickey Mouse. Her younger sister was the one who came up with the name "Goofy." Their father had resisted the name, eventually calling him "Kuffi." The dog was a magnificent intelligent creature and once, when Lilli was still a child, had saved her life.

She could still remember every detail of her misadventure. When the Alster had frozen over, she simply had to go ice-skating. First, she saw cracks in the ice that had spread out like a spider's web, and then felt a painfully-paralyzing cold that took her breath away and swallowed her. When she thought back, she could hear the dog barking. She had reflexively closed her eyes, and when she opened them just as the deadly cold blackness enveloped her, she was overwhelmed by a searing pain that instantly went from her eyeballs to her brain. And she was struck by the daylight shining through the hole in the ice overhead, a bright green with silver air bubbles. It seemed so marvelous that she ignored Goofy's barking on the shore and sank deeper. The next thing she noticed was that the cold encased her like a straitjacket and took her breath away so that she thought she was suffocating. From down below, she had looked up and simultaneously heard her dog's muffled barking and seen his head. The ice skates on her feet obstructed her, but she thrashed about so violently that she was able to rise a bit toward the surface. It frightened her that her clothing (that didn't protect her from the hideous wet cold) had become such a weight, but she was able to reach the surface and catch her breath. She only saw Goofy fleetingly but heard him barking that much louder and instinctively reached for the ice at the edge of the hole, but no sooner had she grasped it, than it broke off. She panicked just as the dog leaped onto the ice and kept barking. Now she thrashed about in terror, but realized that she was slowly losing consciousness. She tried to get to the surface of the ice one last time and thought she was sinking when she suddenly felt ground under her skates. Incredulous, she realized that the water now only reached her chest. With his barking, Goofy had led her to a shallower spot. She strained to fight her way behind the barking dog through the ice to the riverbank. When she climbed out of the Alster, she dropped down onto the snow.

The dog had stopped barking, licked her face, and silence enveloped her. At first, she didn't know if she was still alive or already dead. A woodpecker drummed away, which made everything seem even more miraculous. She saw a swarm of white butterflies—but it had actually begun to snow, and the butterflies were snowflakes.

At home, she downplayed everything, in any event, the only person in the house was the "Aunt"—as they called the maid in those days—and she was cooking, so Lilli was able to change clothes quickly and put everything in the washing machine.

From then on, she loved Goofy even more. But under no circumstances was she going to let herself be afraid of the water. In the summer she bathed more often than before in the pool. She also continued to accompany her father on his sailing expeditions—but without ever attempting it alone. At the age of fourteen, she bought a poster of Caspar David Friedrich's *Monk by the Sea* that her father (who, like her mother, knew nothing about her mishap) had framed and hung on the wall in her room. And around the same time, she learned the names of rivers, lakes, and oceans from an atlas. She was interested in everything that had to do with water. She also loved to join her parents on the Adriatic, and especially in Venice where the sea was "like a breath of fresh air," as she had written in her diary. Her mother was impressed by her daughter's geographic knowledge. She told Lilli various stories of discoveries, and bought her the book *A Voyage Round the World* by Georg Forster.

Several times Lilli accompanied her mother on trips to other countries. While in high school, Lilli would lie down on the floor of the Gallery of Maps in the Vatican to memorize the illustrations. During their fourteen-day sojourn, she had spent five in the Vatican, and each time had stopped in the Gallery until she could see the walls with her eyes closed. Fortunately, her mother was pleased, and so had left Lilli alone with her map study and only picked her up at a predetermined time at the main door to St. Peter's. A year later, Lilli had begun to write in her diary on a regular basis. She recalled two entries: "I am flawed and ridiculous. I remember embarrassing moments too often." And: "My future destiny founders in my desire for fairy tales."

Initially she tried studying law, something her father had insisted upon. She had earned pocket money on the side by drafting legal bulletins and court reports until she worked exclusively for a newspaper. She was passionately interested in what was going on in people's minds—especially when they were in a mental crisis. Most of all, she had determined that most considered themselves victims of circumstances, and the defense attorneys' often patently absurd excuses, as well as the no-less-absurd accusations of the prosecutors seemed to her as if they were inventions of Franz Kafka. Following a protracted argument with her father, she had then begun to study art history. At the time she had become acquainted with the paintings of Maria Lassnig whose work she followed from then on. The painting that occupied her most was the naked woman with pistols in her hands, titled *You or Me*. As soon as she saw it, she knew it applied to her. In a radical way, it illustrated her emotional world, the eternal decision between murder and suicide, because one weapon was pointed at the viewer, the other at herself. Later, Klemens had felt as moved by the picture as she. Everyone was in the same situation: they either had to protect themselves or give up their inner self. It was an inner image that couldn't be more genuine: living dead or in resistance, that's how she interpreted it. Her parents' house, her relatives, school, her classmates, teachers, administrators . . . she would always prefer to disappear than to accept her marching orders. For Lilli, Maria Lassnig was a female Francis Bacon—not simply his successor, but his counterpart. She portrayed the condition of each individual's self-defense that prevails from birth on—Bacon, on the other hand, depicted the brutality of a mankind trained to become victims. Time after time, Maria Lassnig had revealed the existential nakedness. The ugliness of a naked body was everyday banality, the everyday banality ugly. Beauty was overlooked or considered a sacred phenomenon, since everyday reality was a hellish phenomenon. A grimace had been the true facial expression for Maria Lassnig—however, our "normal" "everyday" expression was merely a disguise. Lassnig featured the

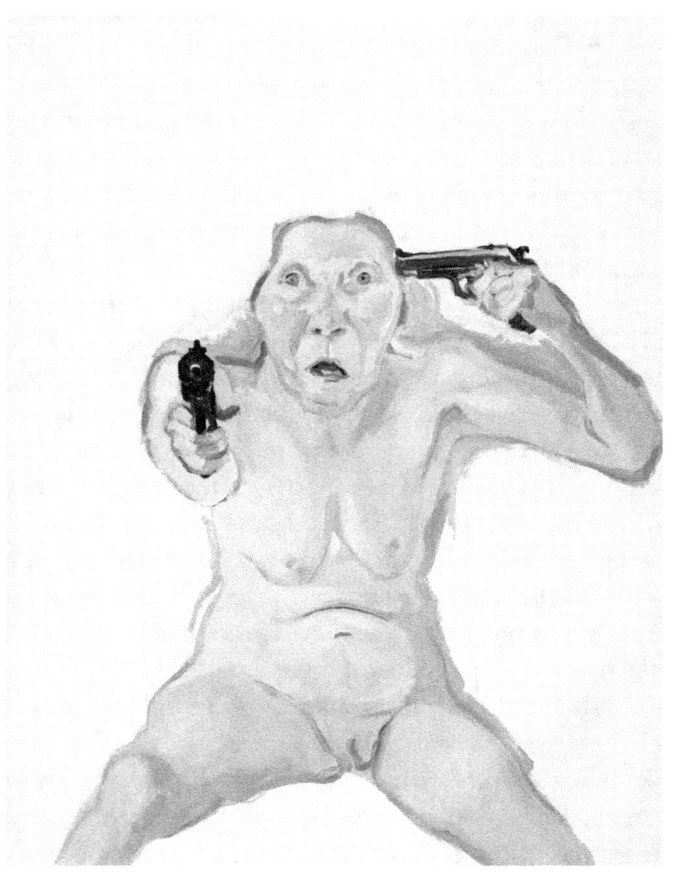

world of ideas, thinking, her invisible inner world and the unknown as true reality. Lilli had planned to write a book about her in the coming years, and now reaffirmed her original intention.

For some time, Lilli hadn't understood herself any longer. It was entirely possible that she had never understood herself. In any event, she couldn't understand the person she had been, nor the person who she was at this moment.

It had been dark outside for some time. She briefly went to the bathroom and then back to bed. In her loneliness—that she felt more frequently and more intensely—she had begun to speak silently with God. He had answered her just as silently. He was extremely wise, she now felt, and helped her with His rare answers. The only thing that upset Him was that she considered herself an atheist.

Lilli loved the night. Just outside the window, the black ocean water—like sleep. You could dive into either one and suddenly see creatures that seemed entirely alien . . .

A lightning bolt made her glance out the window, thunder followed in the same breath. She thought it sounded like two moving vans colliding and the heavy furniture pieces inside them flying in all directions. Then it was quiet again. And it hadn't begun to rain . . . In Hamburg, on the other hand, it had frequently rained often and hard, and it was often foggy . . . just as it had been, several years ago, when she had gone out to eat with her mother.

Her thoughts strayed.

In recent years, while studying in Vienna and writing court reports for a newspaper, she had met her "old lady" less frequently. Toward the end, she had seemed austere and embittered. She had been unfriendly to the waiter, and, after having invited Lilli and thus settling their entire bill, had left only a 75-cent tip, so that Lilli had discreetly slipped him a 10-euro bill. Her husband, Lilli's father, divorced her—but she didn't want to talk about it. Her husband had always had his affairs, but this time he had fallen in love with the owner of a beauty salon who—already divorced herself—had married him that same year. Those had been depressing months for Lilli, too. It wasn't just her parents' marriage that dissolved, but the solidarity of the family, because her younger sister, Isabella, had remained in the villa with her father and his second wife—he had bought a four-room apartment in Eppendorf for her mother. After moving out, she would call her former husband only "Bobo" and the younger daughter " Fuffi," and in return, Isabella had called her an "old frigate." Lilli's older sister Gabriele, on a study-abroad trip to America, had met an auto dealer and married him. Since the parents' divorce, she had spoken only with her mother and invited her to come to America. Lilli was surprised to learn how little Gabriele had liked their father, as she was no longer interested in him, but she did manage to maintain a casual friendly relationship with her sisters.

In any case—as her thoughts returned to their mutual dinner in Hamburg—as usual, her mother had been upset that culture and religion were "becoming extinct." She was angry, but Lilli understood that she was filled with hate as a result of the divorce. Lilli suspected that her mother was possibly trying to rehabilitate her personality through rage, because all of her female friends were bitter, lonely, older women. Again, Lilli was reminded of Maria Lassnig's picture *You or Me*. In her youth, her mother had probably lost her self—or had it taken from her—and now had to learn that she was all alone. She had gradually composed herself, since she felt that Lilli took her seriously. In retrospect, Lilli was convinced that was how she felt. Talking had relieved her mother, serving as confirmation of her significance. On this particular evening she had even seemed cheerful at times, but since the divorce she didn't seem to trust her luck. Now and then she became angry again, but Lilli made an effort to make her happy: she worked herself into a conversational frenzy, sharing intimate thoughts and feelings with her mother. That was their last meeting to date . . .

Lilli's thoughts bounced back again to her childhood and youth. After the fall through the ice, she never went ice skating again, instead she would go roller skating in the summer. Her route took her along the Alster or around the mill pond in the park. She still loved her childhood home, the garden, birds and fish, insects and plants. Her older sister, Gabriele, was more interested in fashion, but Isabella wanted to become a nurse, though her mother corrected her each time: "No, a doctor . . ."—sometimes adding "or a veterinarian."

In summer the family would travel to Venice, to the Lido, and during overcast weather, her parents would take them to the museums in the city: and once to the Accademia that her mother loved. She was excited to show Lilli the works of art, but there were

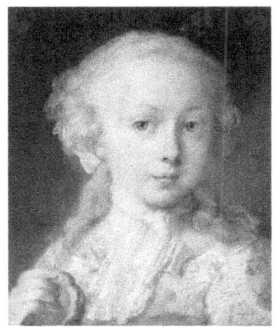
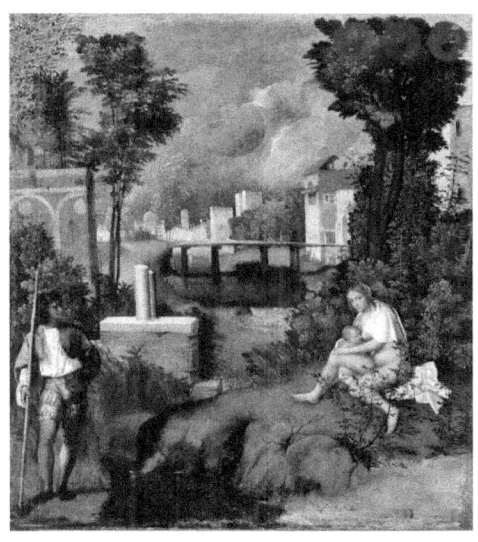

only two that remained in her memory: Rosalba Carriera's *Young Lady of the Le Blond Family* and Giorgione's *The Tempest*. Until now, she couldn't have told you why. She also loved St. Mark's Basilica—not as some sacred place, but because the giant incomprehensible mosaics on the walls and ceiling simply hypnotized her. She couldn't stop staring, she thought they were actually pictures from a different world that was invisible to her. It was their beauty that pervaded and permeated her from all sides. In the winter of that same year, as she accompanied her father to a convention in Paris, she saw the Picasso Museum and Auguste Rodin's *The Gates of Hell*. At the sight of these artworks, she realized for the first time what that "second world" really meant to her. It emphatically proved that she existed. But before she could bring this world to life within herself on a permanent basis, she turned seventeen, became pregnant, and had to abort the "fetus" at the insistence of her parents and out of consideration of the fact that she was still in high school. Her partner had been a classmate, they had attended a ball and gone home directly afterward around midnight. They had only been alone for an hour in the attic of the single-family home—and been terribly afraid that his parents would discover them. However, this secret lust-driven sexual act always remained in her memory as an ecstatic sexual experience; in retrospect, though, it seemed too dangerous, so she never had other affairs with class-mates. When she began to study law, at her parents' urging, and didn't miss an opportunity to visit a museum or a gallery, she had a modest love affair with a theology student that her mother had introduced her to. She had believed that he could initiate her into mysticism, but he knew even less about it than she. She broke up with him the minute he confessed he wanted to abandon his study of theology so that he could make plans with her for a future together.

She studied law with great enthusiasm and little interest, believing that adult life was basically boring and sterile, like the material they had to learn for their exams. Nevertheless, she acquired skills that later helped her get along . . . One day she met Albert who was studying art history. She was in a relationship with him for two years, and wasn't only in love with him, but with his major as well, so she also began to study art history, against her father's wishes. By the time she finished her Ph.D., Albert had already been dead for six months. She hated that she was now reminded of his death. Albert had collapsed from the excessive heat on one of his hikes on the Lüneburg Heath (that he usually took alone) and died in the hospital that same day. She had continued her fascination with art, but one day, when she got an offer from a journalist with a Hamburg weekly newspaper (with whom she had been living at the time) to do an extensive report on a court trial, she accepted. The trial centered on a child killer. From then on, she reported as a freelancer on other spectacular proceedings that she followed with rapt attention. Each of these cases convinced her that she was learning more and more about human existence. Her parents hadn't approved of this new twist in her professional life, but her incisive depictions and analyses did impress them over time.

In the meantime, she had concluded her affair with the journalist . . . She now recalled her first encounter with Klemens . . . It had been in Vienna, in the Kunsthistorisches Museum. On the last day of her week-long sojourn, she had become his lover.

He told her over the phone that, on the day of her departure, he had been overwhelmed, "like a seizure," by a creative urge: in just two months he drew the graphic novel *Hölderlin* and sent it to a Hamburg publisher, as Lilli had advised. She eventually introduced him to the publisher who brought the book out six months later. By this time, Klemens regularly commuted back and forth between Vienna and Hamburg. But now things began to change for Lilli as well. When her parents met Klemens, they were wary at first, but after the *Hölderlin* comic book came out, they got along better. For his part, Klemens was attracted to her family's name, Kuck—especially because of its similarity to "Kuckuck," the name of the cuckoo bird, as he used to say. He voraciously read scientific treatises on the cuckoo and told her the name, in some cryptic way, fit her father (which Lilli avoided mentioning to him). Klemens described himself as a cuckoo child. They had been together for months when Lilli learned that Klemens had been adopted and didn't know who his real parents were. Later, he had only spoken of "foster parents" who had lived in rural Styria.

One day they had traveled together to Caputh on Lake Schwieloch on the Havel River. They had visited Einstein's vacation home and the Einstein Tower in Potsdam. He was also allowed to go sailing with a Caputh local, just as Einstein had done. During subsequent reading in an Einstein biography, Klemens learned that following the scientist's death, the attending medical examiner, Harvey, had removed the physicist's brain and kept it alternatively in his garage and in his house for forty years. In *Driving Mr. Albert*, he found a thorough description of a journalist's journey to deliver the man's brain to Einstein's daughter. This, together with *The secret Life of Albert Einstein*, brought him to write a graphic novel about the famous man's life, particularly with access to the physicist's letters, his well-known sayings, and to his encounters with other famous scientists. Klemens worked on this comic book for two years, and when it came out, his publisher sold the rights "worldwide." He continued to draw and write comics for children, but his next major project was focused on "Jack the Ripper," where he relied on Patricia

Cornwell's theories of who Jack the Ripper actually was. She had identified the famous German-English painter Walter Sickert as the true murderer. Klemens went to England twice, joined a tour "On the trail of Jack the Ripper," photographed the murder scenes, watched the movies and documentary films, and made drawings and sketches for nights on end. The case involved thirteen women who were murdered, in addition to the attempted murders of women who survived. Cornwell had specifically suspected the painter based on his series of paintings entitled "The Camden Town Nudes"— bleak renderings of a man and a woman in miserable bedrooms in the district where the murders had taken place. Sickert had lived in Camden Town for many years. But Klemens was most drawn to the artist's paintings of Venice and his style that bordered on Impressionism and Modernism. For his purposes, Klemens had transported the murders to Hamburg in the 1930s and invented a painter as the killer. The comic book was translated into Japanese, English, French, and Italian. In the meantime, he sold the house in Styria that he had inherited from his deceased foster parents and spent more and more time with Lilli in Venice, as he intended at some point to publish a graphic novel about Casanova, based on the man's six-volume autobiography. For her part, Lilli's enthusiasm for art had been reignited by their many trips together, she quit her job at the Hamburg weekly and, instead, wrote entries for exhibition catalogues in the Hamburger Kunsthalle. A bit later, she applied for a position at the Kunsthistorisches Museum in Vienna and was hired almost immediately.

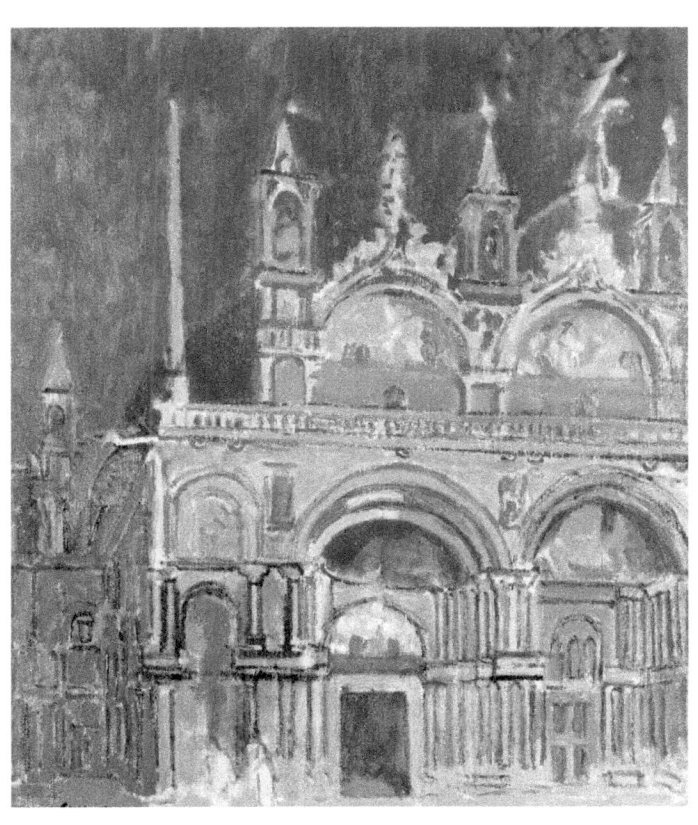

13
A View of Things

After breakfast, she didn't waste time worrying whether Commisssario Zacchini would phone her or not. And she wasn't going to wait for someone or other to show up at the Museo Ca'Rezzonico at 2 p.m. as the message from the pension's porter had requested. She'd had enough bad experiences from anonymous tips. Perhaps someone wanted to use her as bait for something, she thought, or maybe just lead her around by the nose.

She had a great view from the breakfast room out to San Giorgio Maggiore, and she instinctively decided to enjoy the view from its bell tower.

She waited for the vaporetto at the San Zaccaria station, and in just a few minutes she arrived at the small island with its Benedictine abbey. Since she didn't care to see the church consecrated to St. George, and the elevator was only accessible from the store, she tried to find another route to the elevator. At the turn to the entrance, she recoiled at the sight of a huge weathered figure with a halo, almost black, but with angel's wings. She immediately thought "Angel of Death." But a photograph with text informed her that this was the old angel that had previously graced the peak of the tower. On a framed sign beside the photograph, she read that the tall bell tower had originally been part of the convent church on San Giorgio Maggiore. It had collapsed and, after more than 300 years, been rebuilt as a small-scale replica of the campanile at St. Mark's . . . Lilli thought about long winter nights, about bad weather and heat, about strong storms, and just had to touch the figure.

A priest held a block of tickets for the tower in one hand, euro-bills in the other, and was trying to stuff as many visitors into the elevator as possible. Lilli seriously considered turning back, but since she was in line, she remained passive, allowed herself to be crammed into the elevator with the other tourists, and once up in the tower, was shoved out into the open. As soon as she was able to squeeze into a vacant spot on the mesh-enclosed platform, she enjoyed the truly magnificent view of St. Mark's Square and the Lagoon. She gazed down on the idyllic harbor for sailboats, the incomparable landscape and city, and imagined that she could fly. She also noticed on the ground a labyrinth of pruned shrubs that instantly aroused her curiosity. She couldn't take her eyes off it. Last of all, a young woman pointed out the Cana Orfano to her female companion. Because the woman spoke English, Lilli was able to understand that, in earlier times, criminals who had been condemned to death by drowning, were executed here at night.

She rode back down in the "pigpen elevator," as she silently called it. When she entered the shop, she inquired if it was possible to see the labyrinth (which had fascinated her) up close. Lilli had to wait a quarter of an hour for the next tour; in the meantime, she bought a postcard of the "Angel of Death," a ticket for the tour, and was given headphones that would acoustically guide her in German through the cloister. A pleasant young woman accompanied the small group. Lilli learned that the garden, the "Labirinto Borges," had been completed in honor of the twenty-fifth anniversary of the death of the Argentine writer, Jorge Luis Borges. Over circuitous routes through the cloister, they reached a terrace directly overlooking the labyrinth. She heard the anonymous voice in the headphones say that more than 3,000 boxwood trees had been planted that now had grown to an average height of 5½ feet and were trimmed to keep the hedges from casting large shadows: if you concentrated, you could make out numerous symbols in the plant labyrinth. The young woman then explained isolated shapes, such as "the walking stick" or "the mirror." The voice in her headphones went on, stating that Venice itself was a labyrinth. Jorge Luis Borges had "loved" the Italian city more than anything else. The garden had also acquired the name "The Garden of Forking Paths," after Borges' short story of the same name. Since the writer was blind in his old age, the labyrinth also represented a monument to the blindness of mankind. At the entryway to the cloister, you can read the name of the labyrinth in Braille, as well as the complete short story "The Garden of Forking Paths," Lilli learned.

She alertly studied the garden, laid out in "secret writing" and bordered by a row of cypress trees that formed a natural fence. Gradually she understood that the bushes of one half of the labyrinth formed the name BORGES, and the opposite side mirrored this. It was like the brain, she thought, "symmetrically identical." In addition, the headphone commentary pointed out that a concrete surface made it impossible to plant the boxwood trees directly in the ground, so they had been set in three-feet-tall dirt-filled containers, that left the impression they were swimming on the concrete surface. It seemed to Lilli as if she herself was moving, floating over an open book, and she understood that inscrutability is the only true certainty on this earth. The voice in her headphones was just explaining that the form of the letter "O," as if mirrored on two facing pages, represented an hourglass and thus symbolized the passage of time. Suddenly, Lilli saw Klemens' mirror writing, but, like the garden labyrinth, it revealed just as little about the puzzles that surrounded it and only added another riddle to the earlier one.

Strangely tired, she made her way back to the vaporetto station. A strong breeze had come up, and ruffled her hair. She hadn't felt the wind within the walls of the convent and was uneasy at first. Confused, she initially took the vaporetto sailing in the opposite direction to La Giudecca. Once there, she got off at the Zitelle station and waited for the next waterbus that brought her back.

The waiting platform, where she was now alone at noon, rocked more vigorously than usual. She imagined she was living in a swaying cottage, with furniture, a bed, and kitchenette that tumbled all over each other: Goofy the dog, her phonograph records, pictures, telephone, silverware, wall clock, mop, her books and clothes . . . On one of her trips to Venice that she had undertaken alone, she recalled she had encountered a homeless man in the waiting platform on Zattere. He had just put a bottle of alcohol back in his jacket, and the waves swayed him . . . into the abyss . . . or into wild dreams . . . or into a nap.

Just then she saw the huge white cruise ship, a swimming "skyscraper," slowly approaching, as if it wanted to crush her. She had stood up, had held on to the doorway that faced the water, and cushioned the ever-increasing waves with her knees, when she felt a blow to her back, lost her balance, dropped her purse, and fell into the water. It instantly brought back memories of falling through the Alster ice—she fought to keep her head up, and stared at the white wall that was the cruise ship, passing before her very eyes, and when she looked around in panic, she spotted a figure in jeans, a green T-shirt, sneakers, and a black woolen cap who was just running off with his head down. The waves were now so powerful that she was only able to reach the shore with great difficulty and needed an extra effort to pull herself up, while still struggling to catch her breath. She was finally lying on the shore, puffing, but hurried to the waiting platform to try and find her purse that she had dropped. It was obvious that she had been deliberately pushed, and Klemens had probably been deliberately pushed too, when he fell on the stone bridge.

Fortunately, her purse was still lying on the floor of the strongly-rocking waiting platform. The man was nowhere in sight. He wanted her to drown in the canal, no doubt about it. Shivering from the cold, she raised her head and now saw the waterbus steadily approach the station. Her breathing had settled down, and—drenched through and through—she didn't care how she looked, she was only thinking about the Pensione Wildner and the police. The alarmed conductor on the vaporetto asked her something in Italian and reached out to steady her as she boarded. She just stood there, as the water dripped onto the deck from her clothes, her hair, and her body. A curious couple who watched her from a safe distance, whispered to each other and turned away when Lilli stared back at them, while the conductor again asked her something in a concerned tone of voice. She wasn't exactly cordial when she indicated that she didn't understand him and was also freezing, because it took her a great deal of effort to keep her teeth from chattering. She was finally able to get herself under control and plop down on the next-best seat in the nearly-empty cabin. With all her physical and emotional aches and pains, she also felt a nameless rage against everything. She thought of the three Erinyes, Greek goddesses of vengeance with snake-hair and eyes dripping poisonous drool or blood, as she fought against her wildly chattering teeth. She told herself that, as far as she was concerned, she would have to leave the Pensione Wildner and, like Klemens, move into the furniture store with Lisa and Nicole Alberti. As she disembarked, she noticed that people were secretly laughing at her or that she was otherwise causing a commotion. Without looking back, she ran to the Pensione where the porter asked her in English if it was raining or had rained.

In her room, it took her another hour to calm down. Of course, it was better if she phoned Commissario Zacchini and then left. But she had the feeling that it wouldn't take much to get the ball rolling again. And she wanted to be in Venice when they caught Klemens' killer. Maybe it was the same young man who pushed her into the water?

Her decisiveness soon became indecisiveness. The only thing she knew for sure was that she wouldn't keep the appointed meeting at the Ca'Rezzonico. She didn't feel hungry or thirsty. And she would report to the police. But then her intention vanished into thin air. The best thing would be if she were drunk.

She took out her laptop and wrote an e-mail to Commissario Zacchini in which she told him everything (well, most everything) that she hadn't mentioned before—starting with her encounter with Galli, about the story with Guido Alberti, up to what she had learned about Signor Blanc in Sant'Erasmo, but without mentioning any names—with the exception of the woman lawyer. At the end, she wrote that she had been pushed into the water at the Zitelle station. The only thing she still kept secret was her meeting with Galli at the cloister island of San Lazzaro degli Armeni.

It took her an hour to finish her summation, and by then she really was hungry. She ordered room service to bring up spaghetti with calamari and water, got a bottle of wine from the refrigerator, and felt she was regaining her strength. She didn't send her e-mail until she left the room. She didn't plan on ever returning to the Pensione, but she did leave her luggage, as Galli had recommended, taking only her purse with her.

She had just reached the street when she noticed two men who seemed to be watching her. She ignored them until she got to the arcades at the Doge's Palace where she only saw one of them. Since he was inconspicuous, she kept going. She had no idea of where she would spend the night: in Alberti's furniture store? In a hotel at the Rialto Bridge? She had money, and since she had been Signor Blanc's guest at the Pensione Wildner, she hadn't had to surrender her passport at the front desk.

Shortly after leaving the arcades, she once again saw the man who was apparently following her. She hurried past St. Mark's Basilica, ducked into one of the narrow alleys, and found a bar she had patronized on an earlier visit. It was a dark place with few customers. In the back room she realized she was alone and wasn't sure if that was good or bad.

The opposite wall was almost completely covered with old framed black-and-white photographs that extended down to the table top. She ordered a spritz and distracted herself with the photographs: *acqua alta* at the Rialto Bridge that was frighteningly deep, *acqua alta* at St. Mark's with gondolas and people, and then the huge pile of bricks and building debris lying in the middle of St. Mark's following the collapse of the Campanile in 1902 . . . A procession and a huge crowd of spectators at the steps to the Basilica, a paddle steamer at the Piazzetta, people at a canal that was pumped dry, and, finally, fishermen lugging baskets full of marine life across the Piazzetta.

She quickly drank up her spritz, paid, and left—without looking back—for Caffé Florian where she found a vacant table out front in the sunshine. She was glad to see that the head waiter, Roberto, was on duty. He noticed her, quickly jotted down her order—another glass of spritz. Before he hurried off, he bent down and whispered: "Do you see her . . . over there . . . the Japanese woman!" And he indicated a direction with a facial gesture.

She nodded to Roberto, stood up, and went directly between the tables to the foreign woman. The Japanese woman was wearing a stylish extra-large straw hat and sunglasses, her selfie stick was on the chair beside her.

The band was playing Verdi.

"I am Klemens Kuck's widow," Lilli said in English as she arrived at the woman's table. Startled, the Japanese woman stood up and shook her hand.

"I know that Klemens is dead," she said softly. "Someone must have pushed him off the stone bridge at the train station." She took out a handkerchief and impulsively invited Lilli to join her.

A lovely woman, Lilli thought.

"We got along well together," the foreigner began hesitantly, as they sat down. "He wanted to learn everything about the samurai. I don't know how many times we went through the Museo d'Arte Orientale, four or five times. He took photographs and made notes. Every time he discovered something new . . . Do you know the Ca' Pesaro? I mean the two upper floors?"

Lilli shook her head.

"I am a professor for Japanese art, my name is Homare Miyazaki-Henrich. My husband is a jeweler in Heidelberg. We met Klemens on his next-to-last visit in Venice."

Homare suddenly began to sob, she used her handkerchief, and Lilli observed her now without suspicion. The Japanese woman immediately apologized. "I'm crying, and you are the one who lost a husband." She pushed her ice cream aside, indicated to a passing waiter that she wanted to pay, and briefly explained to Lilli: "I have an appointment with Riccardo. I am very sorry."

"Riccardo?" Lilli didn't know who Riccardo was.

Suddenly Homare smiled: "I . . . could . . . show you . . . the . . . Oriental Museum in Ca' Pesaro . . ." She put her business card down on the table.

Lilli nodded.

"Tomorrow?"

"Yes, tomorrow. I'll give you a call."

"Fine," the Japanese woman replied.

Homare stood up, took the selfie stick and her purse, and Lilli watched her hurry off into the crowd.

Just then, Roberto placed her glass of spritz on the table.

"Everything okay?" he asked softly.

Lilli said nothing. This was the first time she had wanted to flee. There was still a light breeze, with seagulls sailing over the Square. She had a snack, drank two more spritzes so she could figure out why she still didn't seem to trust Homare, and, ignoring her arrangement with Homare, decided to visit the Museo d'Arte Orientale, when she saw Klemens again.

It wasn't Francesco Galli, a voice in her head told her.

He was standing in front of the photographer in the middle of the Square. This time there was a different man beneath the black cloth, his body language signaled hostility.

Lilli was so surprised that she could only watch as the photographer leaped up and tried to punch the man in the Panama hat that she thought was Klemens. The man abruptly leaned back so the blow only grazed his head, he stumbled briefly, regained his balance, and though the photographer held his hands in front of his face to protect himself, the man hit him in the eye and then in the nose, causing the photographer to lose his balance and fall backwards into the flash and the camera equipment which then collapsed. A dozen pigeons flew up and squawked in fear. A crowd instantly gathered that blocked Lilli's view.

She indicated to Roberto the banknote that she slipped under the glass table top and ran in the direction that the man had gone. From a distance she could tell that he looked like Klemens when he ran. The sun hat that he had worn on the Square had fallen off his head, she saw it lying on the ground as she ran past, and left it where it was. The man hurried toward the Giardinetti, he was probably hoping to escape on a vaporetto, she surmised.

She abruptly turned around to see that the stranger who followed her to the bar was still behind her. Even though it concerned her that the unknown man was apparently keeping an eye on her, she continued to follow Klemens—or whoever it might be. He had already reached the vaporetto station when a waterbus to the train station pulled in. The man she was trailing disappeared into the ship with the other passengers. At that moment, Lilli could sense that her pursuer wanted to overtake her. Reflexively, she stuck out her leg and tripped the man, lost her balance and stumbled, but she was able to keep running and catch the waterbus before the conductor fastened the security rope so no further passengers could board, and the vaporetto cast off. Out of breath, she clung to the chrome bar on the platform and kept an eye out for her pursuer. He had gotten up off the ground, but barely missed the waterbus and spit in the canal.

She then spotted the man that she had thought was Klemens, sitting in the cabin. He was staring intently out the window. So, he didn't know who she was and what she looked like. Even though she felt exhausted, she remained standing on the platform to see where he got off. Her brain was working a mile a minute, how else to explain why she now was thinking of the *Watchmen* comic book by Alan Moore, especially the "Rorschach" character and the uninterrupted projection and disappearance of Rorschach inkblot tests on his facemask. Klemens had loved the animated cartoon by the same name. She had only seen the movie with him, but soon could no longer establish relationships so the film had dissolved into fragments and eventually disappeared beyond the horizon of her memory. Then, the first time, she asked herself why "Klemens"— that's what she would call him from now on—had punched the photographer at St. Mark's Square. Meanwhile, she saw that he was telephoning with a serious expression. Was Klemens still alive? If he had had a twin brother, she would have known about

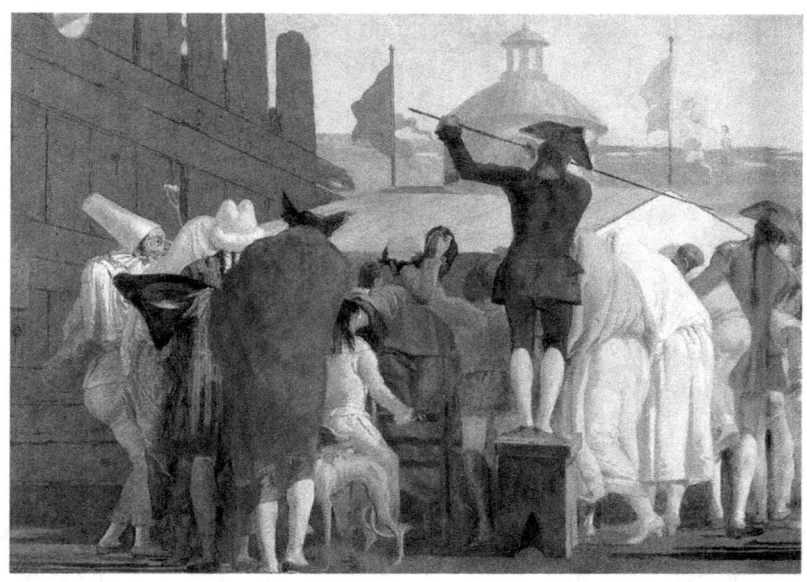

him, because Klemens had often told her about his childhood, but
never mentioned one. And it couldn't really be him, because she
had visited him in the hospital and said goodbye when he passed.
If it was a twin, she would be able to tell by his speech . . . She
suppressed her fears and concentrated on the situation.

To her surprise, the man who looked so much like Klemens got
off at the Ca'Rezzonico station. But he didn't enter the museum of
18th-century Venetian art that was directly on the Grand Canal, but
turned down an alley with a canal and two or three display windows
for antique dealers with parabolic mirrors, commodes, and gilded
chandeliers made of wood. Lilli had never been in this alley. The
man ahead of her—Klemens?—walked past a small rear courtyard
where another antique dealer had displayed his wares. A tabletop
with inlay, a stack of books, a chair, a mirror in a gold frame that
she noticed immediately . . . On the narrow canal, a boat with a
shade sail and vegetable cartons, a man with grey hair at work. The
green water was so calm that the walls of the surrounding buildings
and their windows were reflected in it. Other boats were moored
at the bank. The alley opened up to a square. As she approached,

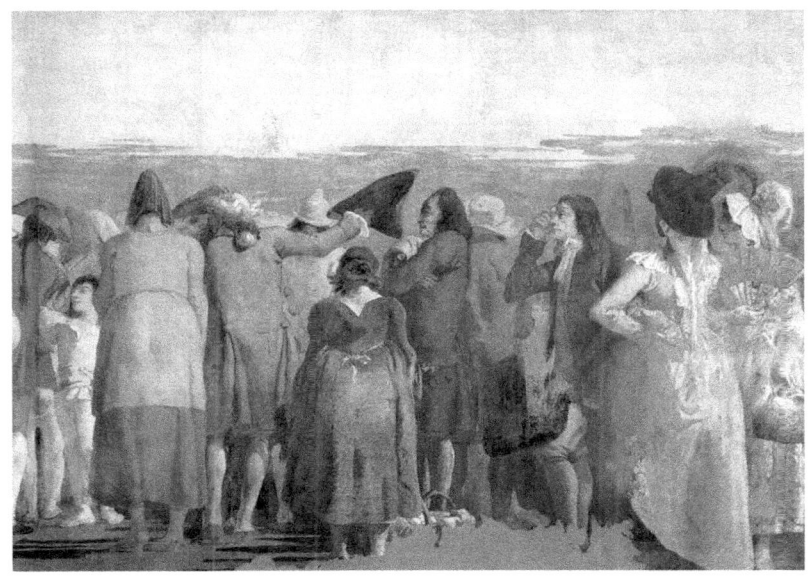

she recognized several market booths that the man passed by. Three of them were selling fish. Large fat gulls strutted over the pavement like roosters at a chicken coop. The merchants would toss them a bit of leftover fish that produced an excited flutter of wings and shrieking. She noticed tin sheets with fish bones, fins, heads and guts that gave off an overpowering smell. A large head with especially large eyes protruded from a pile of dead fish at one of the market booths. When she saw it, she didn't know why it made her think of "Zacchini," and she didn't want to think about it anymore.

She easily followed the man who looked like Klemens, since there was no one about other than the dealers. The merchants were joking back and forth, while "Klemens" walked over to a large poster that depicted Giovanni Tiepolo's *Il Mondo Nuovo*. Almost all the figures were portrayed from the rear. They were waiting by a tent, rich and poor alike, even a *Punchinello*, "Punch," was in attendance. They were waiting to finally get to see pictures from a magic lantern, scenes from the "New World" that everyone was talking about . . . The man she was following had stopped and studied the visualization on the poster . . . It had to be Klemen, Lilli thought—only he would tousled hair also appeared, leading Homare and Klemens quickly to the staircase to the second floor. Lilli knew she had to act quickly. While her pursuer spoke into his phone and disappeared into the store, Lilli hastily bought a ticket at the counter.

In the cloakroom, an overweight woman and an equally overweight man with shoulder-length hair enthusiastically went about their work. Just then a school group came in, the children put their duffel bags on the counter, and the woman worked until she began to pant. At the same time, a girl gave the fat man a very large realistic toy land snail in a transparent plastic bag that the man picked up by his fingertips and took into safekeeping with feigned horror.

Lilli hid in a corner until the school group left to visit the museum, and she joined the group as if she were one of the chaperones. Lilli knew that it was 2 p.m. when she glanced at her wristwatch—the time that the unfamiliar man had invited to meet her at the Ca'Rezzonico. At first, her group was alone. The children had gone up the stairs and visited numerous galleries, such as the Chinese Salon in green lacquer, though most had been inattentive and had to be warned time after time by their two teachers. At Rosalba Carriera's pastels, the older of the two women spoke louder, and the children stopped and were instantly quiet. Lilli went on a few steps ahead of the group to try and find out where the man who looked like Klemens might be—all the while keeping the artist's soft, almost occult portraits in mind. As if they were part of some type of séance, the figures arose from the tapestries. Seen up close, they resembled grainy photographs, but from a little distance, a magic interplay of color, light, and shadows with three-dimensional effects emerged.

Some of the portraits touched her heart. Rosalba Carriera's fate had affected not just her, but Klemens as well. In spite of several painful eye operations, the painter had gone completely blind over the course of five years. By then, she was 76 years old, her mind completely disoriented—in her own words, "in the darkest blackest night." In the adjoining uninhabited Spinet Room, Lilli was suddenly stop to take another look at a painting that he had already seen a hundred times, as if he would never be able to see it again. In the picture, the demonstrator of the "New World" was standing on a chair, wearing a three-cornered hat, giving explanations with a pointer in his hand.

"He's directing the thoughts of his audience," Lilli thought, "or it's a fishing pole and he's fishing thoughts out of the heads of the curiosity-seekers." Supposedly the only two figures in profile were Tiepolo's father (with folded arms) and his son (with spectacles). She knew that the demonstrator was a charlatan who had the curiosity seekers, like marionettes, "dancing to his tune." The spectators, for their part, were starving for daydreams, prepared to be manipulated by these optical illusions, obsessed with the unknown. And they themselves were standing at the edge of the ocean where ships were sailing to the New World or returning from that destination.

She almost didn't notice that she had come to the backside of the Ca'Rezzonico. Lilli acted as if she were searching for something in her purse, as the man who looked like Klemens was greeted at an entryway with a kiss on the cheek from the Japanese woman, Homare. She felt a stab in her heart when she saw this, but in the next instant the two disappeared into the building, and, without thinking, Lilli hurried after them. Presumably he was "Riccardo," with whom Homare had an appointment. All of a sudden, Lilli was standing in the lobby with the old black gondola that she noticed each time she came to visit. The gondola featured a cabin with a window . . . It was a floating palanquin, as she thought in passing, or a giant crow that had been transformed into a gondola.

Homare and "Klemens" seemed to be waiting for someone. It's definitely Klemens, she was convinced. But what was he doing here?

So that she wouldn't be discovered, Lilli hurried to the museum store with her face toward the wall. She just wanted to know what would happen next, but in that moment her pursuer (whom she had tripped near the vaporetto) came in through the glass front entrance, and now Lilli really was frightened. He glanced around, searching, just as an older gentleman with horn-rimmed glasses and

155

so agitated that she had the impression the music instrument in the middle of the room was permeating a sea of billions of reality atoms that, all together, formed the floor, the tapestries, and the ceiling frescoes. Like a dugout canoe, but without visible movement, the spinet was steering toward eternity.

In the next room, a desk that looked like an artistically painted pump organ, and in the room after that a secretary which, in reality, had to be a mysterious triptych with drawers or a commode that resembled an altarpiece.

She had gotten lost, and, in her confusion, she suddenly found an explanation of why she had gotten in this unfortunate state. Her pursuer must have been spying on her at the Pensione Wildner and had followed her to the bar on St. Mark's Square. She next saw him at Caffè Florian. Even though she had no intention of meeting him at the Ca'Rezzonico, she had showed up there, because she had seen the man she thought was Klemens and didn't want to lose sight of him. Yes, she had tripped her pursuer and kept him from taking the same vaporetto with her and Riccardo, but, nevertheless, the man had appeared in the Ca'Rezzonico at the scheduled time in hopes of meeting her . . .

When she reached the gallery with Longhi's paintings, she saw Riccardo at the depiction of the rhinoceros with no horn. Homare had withdrawn, and since Riccardo apparently wasn't certain who she was, Lilli nodded to him when he turned to face her, he said hello, and self-consciously asked if she spoke Italian.

Lilli noticed that he had trouble speaking English. After he told her that he was Klemens' twin brother and she said that she was his widow, he embraced her. Then he showed her his ID, which revealed that he was a policeman. She nodded, relieved. He then waved toward the next room and Homare approached them. Riccardo explained that the two women had, of course, met at the Caffè Florian, and Homare had told him all about it. He took out his smartphone and dialed a number. Before he could speak, the schoolchildren entered the gallery. They raptly stood facing Longhi's paintings, and the younger teacher began to lecture.

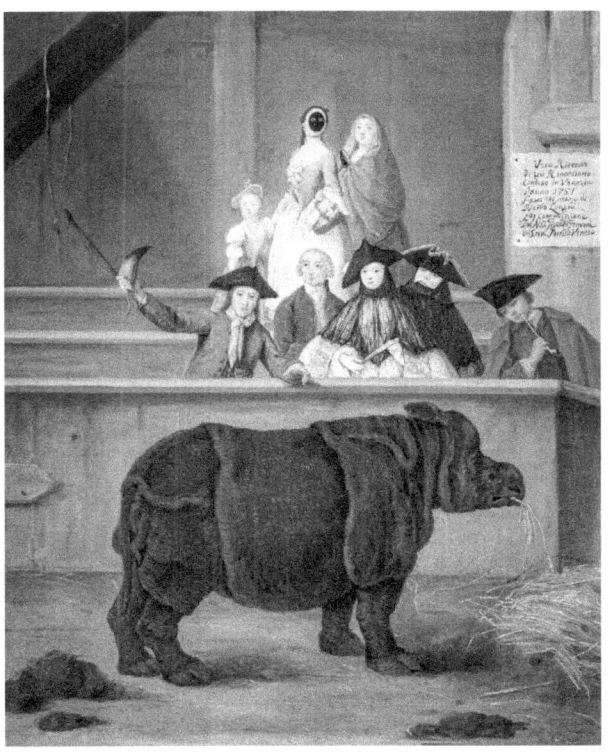

Klemens' twin brother had just completed his brief conversation. He touched her arm and led her into the next room, but before they could speak with each other, Lilli discovered the man who had followed her from St. Mark's to the vaporetto and finally to Ca'Rezzonico. In the next instant, there was a fight, with Riccarco leveling the pursuer. You could still hear the teacher lecturing on Longhi in the next gallery, and then the children's laughter that seemed grotesque to Lilli.

A moment later, Klemens' twin had arrested the man who was just getting up off the floor, put him in handcuffs, while Homare nervously gestured for Lilli to come with her.

Following the Japanese woman, Lilli hastily left the gallery and the museum.

"That was bad," Lilli gasped, and Homare nodded.

They stopped and waited until they had settled down a bit. In the vaporetto they tried to figure out what had just happened. Homare, too, was "flabbergasted," as she herself said—she had forgotten her selfie stick and hat in the Museum.

Later, Homare told her that long ago the Ca'Rezzonico had invited her to give a lecture on Japanese art, and that was when she met Riccardo, Klemens' twin brother. For his part, Riccardo had introduced her to Klemens who had shared his book projects and asked her to explain the objects in the Museo d'Arte Orientale . . . She had worked on a study project about the Museum and for that reason was staying longer in Venice.

In spite of this explanation, Lilli didn't trust her, but she blamed that on the Japanese woman's beauty.

Riccardo and Klemens resembled each other, with minor exceptions. For example, Riccardo had a pigment blemish on the back of his right hand and a small pale scar. That was the first thing Homare noticed.

Meanwhile, Riccardo phoned Homare to say that Lilli shouldn't return to the Pensione Wildner. Her luggage would be brought to her new address.

"And just where would that be?" Lilli asked anxiously.

Homare put her index finger to her lips and glanced suspiciously, first to the left, then to the right. Neither one of them spoke.

Still silent, they got off the vaporetto and made their way, as Lilli realized, to the furniture store. She briefly thought about Nicole and the dead Guido Alberti.

"Is Lisa Alberti aware that I'm coming?"

"Yes . . . Riccardo said that the daughter is looking forward to your visit," Homare responded.

When they reached the furniture store, Homare suddenly said goodbye. Riccardo had only asked her to deliver his sister-in-law to this address . . . For a moment, Lilli was upset.

She then went to the doorbell and rang it. An old woman with a friendly smile, leaning on a cane, gave her a key to the store and, with exaggerated gestures, tried to help her understand something or other. Over and over, she pointed to the furniture store. Lilli thought she understood that Nicole had become sick and that her mother had taken her to see a doctor.

As soon as she had turned on the neon lights, she saw microscopic dust plankton floating in the room. She locked the door behind her, found the hidden bed where Klemens had slept—it was freshly made—turned off the overhead light, switched on the floor lamp, and laid down.

The two notebooks about Klemens' childhood and youth were still in her suitcase in the room at the Pensione Wildner, so she couldn't read what he had written down. She could only remember the sentence: "The first thing I learned about my father was the occasion when the Pope washed his feet." And then the reason why: that this occasion had arisen because one of the prisoners (who had been selected for this ritual) had become sick, and Klemens' father, as a young policeman, was allowed to take his place.

Of course, it made Lilli think about Francesco Galli and what he must have felt, as he experienced this act . . . Then she remembered that—when she was in the furniture store for the first time—she had seen Klemens' suitcase. If she remembered correctly, it was in the small room adjoining the bedroom . . . She stood up and opened the unlocked door. The storage racks were still in place, but now they were empty and Klemens' suitcase was missing. Then she opened the last door, to the bathroom, and there was the suitcase and a large plastic bag with the shirts and underwear that had belonged to Klemens. They had just been stuffed carelessly into the bag. Lilli ignored the plastic bag and pulled the closed suitcase along behind her. She was so moved that she first sat down of the edge of the bed before she opened it. On the very top was yet another notebook, one she had never seen before, she opened it and instantly saw the "usual" mirror script that Klemens had used to create his comics. There were sketches that he had made in the Museo d'Arte Orientale. The book began with the title "Part One." And a picture showed a samurai committing *seppuku*, as ritual suicide is called in Japan, that is, the moment when an attendant, following the detailed ritual, decapitates him from behind. And that was when the story began.

His drawings upset her, but she soon noticed that the text in the speech balloons or on the lower border was frequently represented by key words or was entirely missing, so entire passages were incomprehensible to her. And the manuscript ended in the midst of the action. The final sketches repeated the same scene as at the beginning, featuring the same samurai who had committed seppuku. The caption underneath read: "Part Two." She re-read the text and basically understood that the samurai who had committed seppuku must have had a twin brother who apparently would clarify in the second part what had taken place in the first part. The twin brothers had been strangers who had gotten to know each other through these events. Their bewilderment could be read from their facial expressions, no words were necessary. Evidently the two brothers served the same shogun who ruled his army and his people with benevolence but mysteriously ordered his collaborators to commit murders. No one was allowed to see the ruler's face, he never showed himself, except to his closest collaborators whom he overwhelmed with presents. They told him everything, and he was informed about the slightest detail, but there were seldom instructions. When he nodded, it meant he agreed with his confidantes' suggestions; when he remained sitting and didn't move a muscle, he was allowing them to make the final decisions. He could be absent for long periods of time, such as when he played chess against himself. His clothing was covered with animal designs: with bees, birds-of-paradise, also with foxes, and even with dragons and snakes. As far as Lilli could tell, he acted in ways that couldn't be explained on psychological grounds. His reactions, for the most part, remained mysterious. By the end of the story, all of his confidantes disappeared, they committed seppuku or simply faded away.

From the outset, Lilli had noticed that the man without a face had similarities with Egon Blanc—specifically, with his attributes that she was aware of from various sources . . . And the story of the twin brothers fit in here, too . . .

For Lilli, it was proof that Klemens had artistically processed everything that had happened to him in Venice.

So, the killing of the six policemen must have something to do with Egon Blanc. But there was a great deal of what Klemens had drawn and written that she didn't understand. It was only a draft that she was holding, but she now realized why Klemens had visited the Museo d'Arte Orientale so frequently and met with Homare. Lilli decided not to tell anyone what she had found. She was now very curious to visit the Museo d'Arte Orientale. But first she had to calm down, because her heart had begun to pound. Exhausted, she fell asleep.

14
Japanese Interludes

As soon as Lilli woke up, she set off to visit the Museo d'Arte Orientale. On the one hand, the notebook with the samurai story had made her curious, on the other, she couldn't bear to stay "in the front window of the furniture store," as she called her new home.

Once on the street, she kept looking back to see if there was anything suspicious. She didn't become concerned until, just as the waterbus was about to pull away, a man leaped on board, seemed to be searching around, then remained on the deck and looked through the window into the cabin. She could obviously be mistaken, she thought, but his behavior was unusual in any event. She thought of Homare, and that it would have been better to have called ahead, but still, she wanted to be alone and unobserved. She decided to keep an eye on the man and be obvious about it. With a stern expression, she stared at the window, but the suspect only briefly glanced her way, and then abruptly turned his back to her. But he didn't get off. They sailed past the empty fish hall, gulls flying overhead. Lilli thought about the dossier of the police killings and the hall now seemed like the open jaws of a Leviathan that would devour everything. The pillars were its huge teeth, the orange-colored linen fabric between the pillars its cheeks, the floor its tongue. Only a few fruit and vegetable stands were open. They came to the Rialto Bridge, numerous passengers left the waterbus,

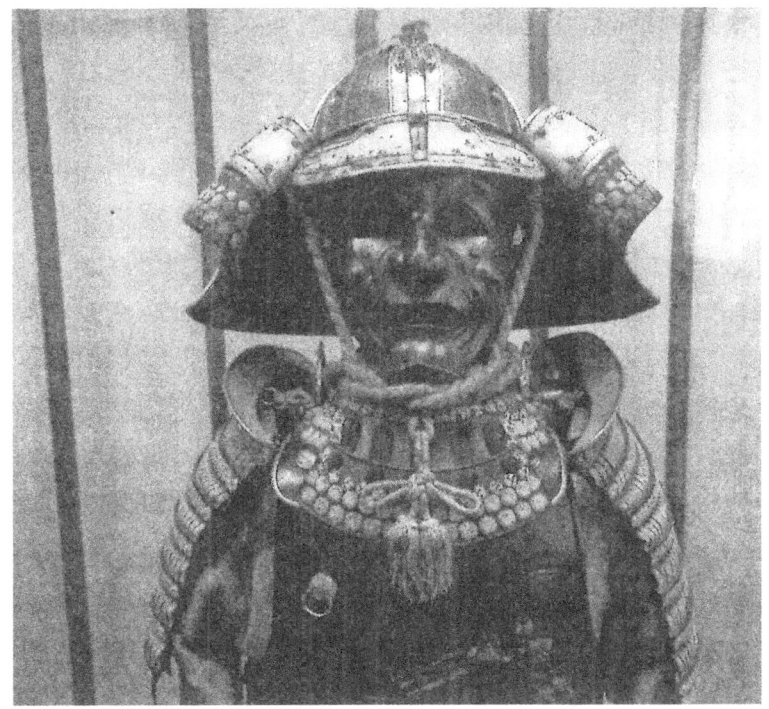

about the same number came aboard. In San Stae, Lilli got off, as planned. She found out that the man had also left the vaporetto and joined a second man who was waiting by a large metal wastebasket.

Lilli made a show of unfolding her city map and studying it until the two men walked past her with impassive faces. As soon as they had disappeared in the alleys, Lilli crossed a placid green canal. Two motorboats, moored to a wall, were completely covered by dark canvas.

She then came to a wall that had large dark spots: white marks and wave formations were barely visible. As it turned out, it was a wall of the Museo d'Arte Orientale that was afflicted by mildew.

There were only a few other visitors. A staff member in uniform complied with her request and led her to the elevator to the fifth floor. She instantly realized the collector's delirium: one item magnetically attracted the next, one similarity spread to another, something new demanded inclusion and immediately branched out into never-before-seen variations. The collection, Lilli read, came from the French ethnologist Henry of Bourbon-Parma who had accumulated Japanese art of the Edo period on a trip around the world . . . One painting even depicted *him* as a samurai.

In the first room, the suits of armor looked like the shells of giant beetles, richly decorated with claws and tentacles, dangerous life-size aliens from outer space with poisonous stingers. With this thought in mind, Lilli turned around, since she had a feeling that someone was watching her. But she didn't see anyone. She stepped back a few feet, glanced in a gallery with 20th-century paintings that she had seen before, but she didn't see anyone here either. She was all alone in the huge upper-stories of the Palace, as if in one of her dreams, she confirmed. As she continued to stare at the suits of armor, they reminded her of combat machines whose only purpose was to destroy and be destroyed, to kill and be annihilated themselves. She imagined she could now grasp the police killings as dream images, without truly understanding them. The appearance of the samurai armor, the helmets with their face masks, expressed ruthlessness, hate, violence, and cruelty. As she broke loose from this vision and climbed a flight of stairs, the "Realm of the Golden Litters" opened up, enchanting and inspiring her. In the display cases and along the walls, she found the most amazing art works that illuminated life and the entire world: saddles where gold-colored dragonflies rested, painted dishes, strange musical instruments, combs, mirrors, tapestries with mysterious illustrations and designs, bowls, busts, furniture . . . A large black-lacquer partition displayed hunters on white horses with animals, primarily rabbits, fleeing, along with a fox. A rider with a dog in his lap chased them. Then Lilli discovered the dead stag on the ground, beside it a hunter with bow and arrow.

Heaven and Hell alternated. In one display case, two angry-looking samurais or shoguns and two humorously-fat cats: their heads white, with "human" eyes and pouting. The animals' bodies and their curled tails were both painted in a gold pattern. Other tiny figurines caught her attention: a monkey was just crawling out of a walnut; a miniature ivory figure was riding on an even smaller cow. Then came the small gallery with a theater for painted puppets. Cardboard demons were arranged on the puppet stage. This time Lilli even discovered on the floor two Buddha figures in the guise of noble princes.

After browsing all the galleries, Lilli just wandered around, leaving to chance and her curiosity where she stopped and stared. She realized that this was more than just a collection of Japanese weaponry and armor, but—and especially—a collection of artfully configured life-defining moments.

At the exit, the grey-haired staff member again offered to take her down in the elevator, and she asked the pleasant old man if there was a café in the building. Lilli made sure that no one was following her, thanked him, and took a seat at the glass wall so she could watch activity along the Grand Canal. She ordered a small bottle of mineral water and Tramezzini and, as she sat there all alone, realized how tired she was. She again grew dizzy, as she had at the Guggenheim Museum.

Outside, heavy rain clouds had formed above the palazzi. Almost in the same instant a bolt of lightning lit up the Grand Canal and its buildings and rain pelted down. At first, the Canal was dotted by the flurry of raindrops in a Pointillist pattern, then small circles and waves developed that swirled the surface and gave Lilli the impression that the Grand Canal was boiling. In the large gallery, the thunder made a loud noise, as if a neighboring building had collapsed, and it seemed she was observing the whole thing as if she were alone in a movie theater. At the first bolt of lightning, all the gondolas had disappeared, and one of the vaporetti was making its way through the roiling waters to the San Stae station. Almost at the same time, another waterbus was leaving San Stae and sailing in the opposite direction. Then, for a long time, nothing happened. The storm moved off as quickly as it had come. The water and the air calmed, and the vaporetti now resumed their casual travels on the Grand Canal. And the clouds no longer hung low and threatening over the palazzi, though it did continue to rain, which forced the gondolas to remain docked. Lilli thought how unpleasant it must be to sit in a gondola during lightening and rain, and to have to wait until you could get off at some pier. The storm gradually transitioned into a steady rain. Lilli had already drunk a second glass of wine and ordered a third when she heard marvelous piano music coming from behind the glass wall of the café. She paid, took her full wineglass out into the atrium that now was like a cathedral, and sat down on a side bench. A woman with frizzy reddish hair, a light-beige jacket slung over her shoulder and a silk scarf around her neck, was sitting at a Bösendörfer grand piano, improvising a seemingly never-ending piece. A half-dozen customers were attending the event. In the large gallery with its multiple echoes, it sounded like the composition of a magical spell, and when Lilli looked up much later, she saw that the old man, listening at the elevator, was the only one left. She finished off her glass of wine and let her thoughts flow freely through her mind. All of her experiences in Venice flashed before her eyes, until she finally realized that she had completely forgotten the island of Lazzaretto Vecchio where Klemens must have visited three times, according to his own notes. Still, she let herself be carried away by the music, until she fell asleep. Actually, she passed out.

15
The End of a Fairy Tale

Lilli stared out the window at the black water, struggled to concentrate, and would have fallen asleep again, but the San Marco station was a place where passengers got on and off regardless of the weather, so she was torn from her snoozing and had to run out into the darkness and the rain. Just as she reached the tangle of alleys at the furniture store, she noticed that someone was waiting at the brightly-lit display window by the front door. He had a suitcase and a travel bag that, from a distance, looked like her own. As she cautiously approached, she recognized Aldrian who, when he saw her, raised his hand in greeting.

He dragged the luggage into the small room and explained that the police were looking for her. Two officers had been assigned to keep her under surveillance, but when Lilli got off the vaporetto at the San Stae station, they had lost sight of her. Now Lilli knew what men he was talking about.

"I've just heard from Riccardo," Aldrian continued, "that Egon Blanc has been flown by helicopter to the Cave Churches of Cappadocia in Turkey. Since nobody knows what might happen tonight, he's asked me to keep you safe."

They quickly left the display window of the furniture store. The sky was still dark with rain clouds, and lightning flared up a sulphury-yellow and then alternated with jet-black.

"Where are we going?" Lilli shouted.

Aldrian pointed to the Lagoon and started to run. They were soon out of breath, but Aldrian didn't stop until they got to the Vallaresso station where a motorboat was waiting for them.

"They've just arrested Hainer," Aldrian yelled, as they boarded the boat. "He's a younger half-brother of Signor Blanc who wanted to take control of the dynasty."

"It was Hainer's plan to have Riccardo, Klemens' twin brother, pushed from the bridge because the policeman had investigated Hainer and was on his trail. But the hitman thought Klemens was Riccardo. We don't know why Klemens was on the bridge. He must have found out that his twin was going to meet Hainer there."

At that moment, the boat left with Aldrian and Lilli on board.

"First we'll head for the Lido and Malamocco," Aldrian said. "That's where the old fortress is, on the island of Lazzaretto Vecchio. We'll spend the night there, until I get word that the police operation is over. The Venetians call the island *Isola del dolore*, "the island of pain," because that's where they brought the dying plague victims. Back then, their death cries could be heard on the Lido, which is only fifty yards away. Nowadays, stray dogs are kept in the hospital."

Lilli remembered that Klemens had told her that in one of his letters.

They reached the dock. Aldrian had a key for the gate in the massive wall, and he put on a headlamp. Then they went down a path, past yellow signs that said *Pericolo!*, "danger!" Ever since they set foot on the island, they could hear dogs barking.

Aldrian led her through the darkness into a high-ceilinged and empty hall, the only light coming from his headlamp. The barking of the caged stray dogs was muted here, so they must be confined on another part of the grounds. In this huge hall lay a stripped white sailboat with a pile of wool blankets inside. The entire furnishings consisted of a folding chair beside two more sailboats without masts.

Aldrian turned off his headlamp.

"Try to get some sleep," he said calmly, pointing to the boat.

In the silence, Lilli could hear the faint barking of the dogs. She closed her eyes and imagined sailing off into the night on the sailboat.

When she opened her eyes, the first thing she heard was the dogs yelping, they were whimpering, they were going wild. "Are they still barking?" Lilli asked herself, "or have they just started up again?"

It was dark . . . "A barn," she thought.

She listened carefully to the barking dogs. She wasn't afraid in her boat. She wondered in which hospital building they were keeping the stray dogs. Were they locked in cages? What would they do with them if no one came to claim them? How could anybody even get on the island to see them? And how many dogs were there?

In spite of her exertion, in spite of her nervous tension, she was no longer tired. Maybe she was just escaping into the world of sleep. She laid back on the blankets and closed her eyes again.

The next time she awoke, Aldrian was sitting on the folding chair, practicing hand movements for some magic trick. He made playing cards disappear and even float in the twilight. She could see it all very clearly, the cards flew like sailing swallows from one hand to the other. He opened both hands and they were as empty as the hall. He then stood up to smoke a cigarette at the other end of the room. As this was happening, she noticed that it was raining. She had the impression that the raindrops were clattering needles that pricked the tin roof, as if old sewing machines were driving their bobbing movements. Suddenly Aldrian began to pull frogs out of his pants pockets, and she realized that she was still dreaming. Only now did she open her eyes.

Aldrian was sleeping on the chair, the dogs were barking less often and not as loud. For a time, she, too, slept on, but in her head the dogs kept barking, and when they let up, the raindrops clattered like sewing needles on the tin roof or against the windows, until the dogs resumed their barking.

It was 5:30 a.m. when Aldrian gently nudged her awake and urged her to join him in going back to the city, to Venice.

169

She struggled to sit up in the sailboat, and determined that the dogs were no longer barking. Had someone retrieved them during the night and taken them somewhere else? Or put them to sleep?

Aldrian had put the headlamp back on and led her through the yellow *Pericolo!* signs to the gate in the wall which he opened and then locked behind her.

16

Lilli

After Lilli had awakened in the hospital from her coma and been treated with an infusion, the following morning she accepted Caecilia Lanz's invitation. For two weeks now, she had been living in a spare room on the island of La Giudecca where she had a view of the Rio del Ponte Lungo. These days she visited the Accademia, the museum for Venetian art, as she always did whenever she was in Venice, and spent a great deal of time with a portable folding altar by Paolo Veneziano that touched her, especially the iconography and fairytale charm of the coloration.

In the museum, she had gone from painting to painting, as if she were viewing stations from her own childhood. She had memories of almost every picture in the enormous exhibition. Many of them had excited her, others not so much. But each time she had eagerly waited to see if her relationship to them had changed.

In an outpatient room at the hospital, Lilli had seen portions of a TV report on the insurrection of Egon Blanc's half-brother that had then mingled with her dreams. For days on end, the front pages of the newspapers were full of photos and accounts.

Riccardo came to see Lilli at the home of the Lanz couple and filled her in on every detail about Jeremias Hainer and his private bodyguards' confrontation with the police. Hainer's people, he said, had tried to storm the Arsenal that was surrounded by 15-feet-high walls. But the police and the army were waiting for them in the darkness and arrested them during the shoot-out. Riccardo had received a glancing wound to his right upper arm. The killer who had shoved Klemens off the bridge at the train station admitted it, was in jail in Mestre, under arrest with another criminal— apparently the guy who pushed Lilli into the water, though she couldn't identify him on a photograph. They had also arrested all the other gang survivors of the gun battle and put them in jail. In total, there were five dead and a large number of wounded.

Riccardo resembled Klemens in appearance, but also in his behavior and interests, sometimes in weird ways. But he was more practical than Lilli's deceased husband. He couldn't draw particularly well, but when it came to telling a story, in retracing or anticipating events, they were like two peas in a pod. He told Lilli that, before he met Klemens for the first time, he'd never heard from him. They had sat in the Caffè Florian, each alone at his own table. Finally, Riccardo stood up and introduced himself, and Klemens, startled and friendly, had shaken his hand. They sat together until midnight, and that was how Klemens had learned they were twins. After an initial shock, they immediately felt affection for each other. Riccardo had told him that for the past twenty years, he, Riccardo, had developed a close relationship with their common father. When Lanz, the translator, had become complicit in murders (that were in some humane way justifiable), Signor Blanc had had it in for the old man.

17
Klemens' Childhood

When Lilli, half-asleep, opened her eyes, she could still envision the first page of Klemens' notebook. The twins' parents had met in Jesolo, she recalled. But after several stolen nights of love, Francesco had taken off. He had given her a phony address in Padua and ended their relationship by his stubborn silence. Francesco knew about the illegitimate twins, but he and Maria had never spoken about it— she, because it was a scandal for her family, he, because he didn't want to have anything to do with it. As she used to say, Francesco never spent "a dime" on Klemens. One Christmas Eve, a pack of English-language Walt Disney comics arrived in the mail from Italy, without a return address or a cover letter, and, as it turned out, forwarded anonymously by Maria. The first Lilli ever heard about it was in Klemens' notebooks. Among them were Tom & Jerry comics and a Pinocchio book in Italian with illustrations by Carlo Chiostri. Then came the first Walt Disney VHS cassette, in Italian with English subtitles—*Alice in Wonderland*—and over the years, *Peter Pan*, *Snow White and the Seven Dwarfs*, *The Jungle Book*, *Dumbo*, as well as *Pinocchio*. Even though he didn't understand the language, Klemens had watched the VHS cassette tapes over and over. This was also how he got to know *Batman*, *Tarzan*, and *Superman* in junior high school. By the time he was eleven, he had already begun to trace various comic-book figures and, eventually, to invent his own (who basically resembled his classmates and teachers).

His adoptive father, Hans Schneider, had been a taxidermist at the Joanneum University in Graz, where—with his stuffed mammals, birds, and prepared butterflies— had inspired Klemens to create new and harmless animal tales and sketches. His adoptive father also taught him about preparing insects (though it disgusted the boy).

His adoptive mother had been a religious woman, had learned to play the violin, and, in her spare time, had listened to the music of Johann Sebastian Bach. At the age of 22, she had begun to play the organ, and five years later was accompanying Sunday services as the organist.

The adoptive parents had been friends with Franz Hofstätter—a hunter and "gendarme," as they called the police in rural areas. He had Klemens' adoptive father prepare the antlers of a deer he had shot. As a boy, Klemens often came into contact with the gendarme, who spoke with contempt about the "riffraff"—burglars, murderers, child molesters, and thieves. Hofstätter was a bit more amusing when he told the boy about a marriage con artist. When he and Klemens would return from a walk in the woods or an outing, and his wife would serve them fruit juice on the veranda, the man would make an exception and talk about convicted criminals. The back wall of the veranda, as Klemens recalled, was covered with trophies: wood grouse and owls, woodpeckers, jaybirds and magpies, but mostly goose wings and deer antlers.

From early childhood, Klemens had to go to church with his mother every Sunday, and from second grade on, serve as altar boy to the absentminded priest during Mass. Klemens soon knew the rituals for weddings, funerals, baptisms and consecrations so well that he could correct the priest in a soft or muffled voice, if the man became confused. As the priest's forgetfulness increased, bystanders were barely able to stifle their laughter.

Klemens gradually realized that his mother's lovely organ music, the songs and prayers of the people in church, were in stark contrast to their normal behavior and their entire lives. He felt the grownups were somehow sinister. Even his adoptive mother's Bible on her nightstand beside her bed was full of violent and scary stories. Since The Son of God, who was himself a god, had been killed by humans, why should he trust them? In the exceptionally large church, they even had a wood Jesus hanging from a cross. Added to that, Klemens regretted the dead animals in his father's workshop and the gendarme's stories. He also had "bad dreams." Where did they come from? he used to ask himself. Even the grownups would complain from time to time about nightmares. Whenever his adoptive mother heard bad news, she had a habit of crossing herself. But he still clung to her.

One day he discovered that he could draw people "right out of his head," especially when he exaggerated their traits. Though he had always been just an average student, people admired his "caricatures," as his mother called his sketches. On the other hand, the essays he wrote for school were always really strange: imaginative, succinct, and as the teacher used to say, on the whole, "exaggerated." In high school he was alternately praised or damned by his German teachers, depending on how each one felt about "childhood" and "inspiration."

Lilli was impressed the most by the drawings that expressed deep fears. His sexual fantasies and thoughts of revenge left her chilled, just as his suicidal thoughts did. She was relieved when she had finally finished the two notebooks about Klemens' childhood that Alberti had sent her.

18
Signor Blanc's Return
And Lilli's Journey Home

At first, she couldn't sleep after reading Klemens' notebooks, but when she awoke, she felt the need to keep reading. So, when Riccardo came to visit and listened to her stories, she found it both helpful and supportive. Riccardo was divorced and didn't have any children. He told Lilli about his life as an undercover cop and his desire to change professions. Soon they were meeting regularly in late-afternoon at the Osteria Zemai behind the Rialto Bridge (that Aldrian had recommended). Sometimes Aldrian and Beatrice joined them, but generally they were alone. When Lilli had finished reading Klemens' notebooks, she felt the need to visit his grave in Vienna. She had found an endlessly-long list of unread text messages and mailbox numbers on her smartphone. But she didn't call anyone. She had only sent two text messages to her sisters: one, that Klemens' killer had been captured; and the other, that she had to stay in Venice for another month. And she also shared that message with the Kunsthistorisches Museum in Vienna.

To everyone's amazement, Signor Blanc announced his return. Contrary to Riccardo's information, he had not flown to the Cave Churches in Turkey after all, but to the fortress-monastery of Sucevita in Romania, its church façade decorated with amazing frescos. The urge to illustrate as many stories as possible has resulted in a "fragmentation" into individual pictures so that deciphering all the stories and details is difficult, as she learned from Caecilia. But apparently that was precisely the reason Signor Blanc loved the fortress-monastery so much.

Prior to his return, according to the newspapers, Blanc had made significant monetary contributions to all the families of the deceased policemen—and Francesco Galli (who had been rehabilitated by the police department and retroactively promoted to the rank of senior officer) had received a similar amount. Riccardo was also promoted, and, in addition, received 100,000 euros for the leading role he had played in the operation. In addition, he was awarded a medal. Though she hadn't expected it, Lilli was also awarded the same amount in the form of a bank check, along with an apology. The remaining aggrieved parties received cash benefits and the police were reimbursed for their involve-ment. Moreover, charitable institutions received significant donations, to their great surprise.

It only took a couple of days until Signor Blanc once again enjoyed great popularity among the residents of the city and the island, even though he had been a participant in these recent events.

A charity event for the surviving relatives of the deceased and for children with Down syndrome had been announced for the coming weekend on St. Mark's Square and in the surrounding cafes. Posters advertised that Aldrian would do his magic tricks in the middle of the Square and all the children would receive presents from him.

Nicole, who (together with her mother) had invited Lilli to lunch one Sunday, couldn't wait. Over the phone, Lisa Alberti had explained to Lilli why Lisa's husband had been killed: as a former tracker and detective, he had gotten involved . . . and the killer himself had been searching for Galli, to win him over as an ally for Jeremias Hainer. As a result, they had crossed paths on Pellestrina.

When Lilli told Nicole that she, too, had a hard time sleeping, Nicole sang:

> "Ninna, Nanna,
> Coccolo della Mamma
> Ninna, Nanna,
> Coccolo del Papa."

Lilli learned that, in English, it meant:

"Sleep,
Mama's little darling,
Sleep,
Papa's little darling."

Nicole and Lilli hugged as they said goodbye, and they cried. Lilli invited Nicole and her mother to come visit her in Vienna.

Riccardo and Lilli had agreed that he would drive her car from Punta Sabbioni to Vienna. In the meantime, Lilli would take a waterbus with Galli to the airport. They had tickets to Vienna, where they would first visit Klemens' grave. In the meantime, according to her father-in-law, as a result of Signor Blanc's financial contribution, Riccardo had resigned from the police department. He had also begun to learn Lilli's mother tongue, Galli told her on the plane. But, he added, learning a language is a tedious journey. Lilli was silent and gazed out the window.

Outside, the snow-covered Alps came into view.

"I wanted to get to the bottom of the truth," Galli said. "But I myself lied time after time. Later on, I learned that the search for the truth had led me astray. And that I didn't begin to understand things, until I started to doubt the truth."

Lilli kept gazing out the window. Somewhere down below, Riccardo was driving her car to Vienna. And she thought that the pictures in the Museum were waiting for her, too.

AFTERWORD
"Love's Labors"

Gerhard Roth was born in Graz, Austria, on 24 June 1942, the son of a physician and a nurse. He studied Medicine at the University of Graz to fulfill his parents' expectations, but quit to work in a data-processing and computing center in order to support his wife and three children. His first publication, at the age of 30, signaled a new trend in Austrian literature and allowed him to focus entirely on his literary craft. His resulting seven-volume cycle, *Die Archive des Schweigens* (The Archives of Silence) dealt with the development of fascism in Austria, and was followed by another seven-volume cycle entitled *Orkus* (Hades) that featured "foreign" crimes, based on his travels to four continents—to the USA, to numerous European countries, then to Israel, Egypt and Japan; his latest cycle is based on many visits to Venice over the years.

Roth is the recipient of almost thirty literary prizes spanning four decades, thus confirming the enduring importance of his work. Along with his devotion to literature, he has frequently been praised (and loudly criticized!) for his political engagement, his outspoken support for social causes, and documentation of crimes against humanity. Gerhard Roth was long considered a controversial writer, often sharply critical of Austria, past and present—a brilliant pariah, a *Nestbeschmutzer*, literally a bird that befouls its own nest. His many awards finally culminated in the Grand Austrian State

Prize in 2016, considered an act of official forgiveness, and certainly long overdue.

Roth has been fascinated to the point of obsession with his country's history, of its collusion with National Socialism, as well as actual incidents such as the disappearance of a Mozart manuscript fragment, the murder of three Chechen refugees, a gas explosion in his own Viennese neighborhood complex—each of which became plots for recent novels.

More recently he has occupied himself with riddles, puzzles, and labyrinths, notably in the earlier novels, *Der Plan* (1998), *Das Labyrinth* (2004) and *Grundriss eines Rätsels* (2014).[1] To extend this labyrinthine motif, the three Venetian odysseys depict the maze of narrow streets and waterways, the encounters with its enigmatic beauty. As Roth has said:

> "Venice is timeless, the city is a revelation, it shows what mankind truly is. Not only history depicts who we really are, it is more evident in art. The true face of mankind becomes accessible, visible and tangible in literature, in architecture, music, the fine arts. I was aware of that when I began my Venice project."[2]

Venice is a showcase for the most noble of human accomplishments. The attractions of Venice for a land-locked Austrian like Lilli (and Roth!) are a vibrant history, impressive

---

1 *The Plan*, *The Labyrinth* and *Artner's Riddle*, all appearing with Ariadne Press.

2 "Venedig ist zeitlos, die Stadt ist eine Offenbarung, sie zeigt, was der Mensch wirklich ist. Nicht nur die Historie stellt dar, wer wir in Wahrheit sind, viel mehr noch die Kunst. In der Literatur, in der Architektur, der Musik, der Bildenden Kunst, wird das wahre Gesicht des Menschen nachlesbar, sichtbar und fühlbar. Das war mir bewusst, als ich mit dem Venedig-Projekt begonnen habe." In: Sven Hanuschek, "In der Kunst wird das wahre Gesicht des Menschen nachlesbar," in: *Frankfurter Rundschau*, 6 Juni 2019.

palaces and villas, official buildings and tony restaurants populated with romantic Italians and exotic foreigners, canals that serve as the main thoroughfares with vaporettos and gondolas for transportation, a maze of narrow streets and alleys requiring a map for orientation with remarkable but out-of-the-way sites such as museums, libraries, bookstores . . . and even a madhouse!

However, below the surface lurk the most despicable traits of our species. As Roth has emphasized:

> "That's where the negative side of humanity plays a larger role. Venice was frequently afflicted with the plague, there's a marvelous archive about it that I was allowed to see. It also deals with the prisons and executions sites. Two pillars of the arcades on the second floor of the Doge's Palace are painted red. Between them the death sentences were read out. Then, on the Piazetta between the familiar pillars with Saint Theodore and the St. Mark's lion, and in accordance with the judgement, the delinquents were skinned or subject to all sorts of cruelties before they were beheaded. For that reason, many Venetians won't walk between these pillars."[3]

3 Heinz Sichrovsky, "Gerhard Roth: "Da komme ich mir geschützt und vergessen vor," in: *news/at*, 23 January 2021. "Da nimmt die negative Seite des Menschen auch eine größere Rolle ein. Venedig war häufig von der Pest betroffen, es gibt darüber ein großartiges Archiv, in das ich Einsicht nehmen durfte. Es werden auch die Gefängnisse und die Hinrichtungsstätten behandelt. Zwei Säulen des Arkadenganges im ersten Stock des Dogenpalastes sind rot angestrichen. Zwischen ihnen wurden die Todesurteile verkündet. Die Delinquenten wurden dann auf der Piazetta zwischen den bekannten Säulen mit dem Heiligen Theodor und dem Markuslöwen entsprechend dem Urteil gehäutet oder allen Grausamkeiten der Folter unterzogen, bevor sie geköpft wurden. Viele Venezianer gehen deshalb nicht zwischen diesen Säulen hindurch."

Venice is thus the product of the entire scale of human endeavor, a reflection of the individual humans that formed it.

The Venice Trilogy

Roth is a realist in the grand tradition. Familiar locales and well-known architectural landmarks are described in detail, placing us in recognizable landscapes and thus cementing his fiction in a convincing and thus acceptable reality. There is no omniscient narrator. The entire novel is told in the third-person from the main character's perspective, based solely on her experiences and perceptions, her hopes and fears. Readers are limited to and thus dependent on Lilli's interpretation of events, since we experience them simultaneously with and through her; we can then judge her responses and the results. There are outside entities that may provide a supplement to her perception of reality, such as newspaper articles and information from others, in addition to real-life events—for example, an actual tornado and the gun battle with an implied Mafia group—that corroborate her reality and thus support the narration.

Roth's novels feature individuals who are forced out of their professional and everyday routines and must deal with unexpected, often life-threatening situations. Their previous training and lifestyle do not prepare them for these encounters, so they must adapt as best they can, by retreating or confronting the threat, thereby facing defeat and perhaps even death. In the present trilogy, three Austrians come to Venice, witness killings, become targets themselves, and must respond if they hope to survive the threats to their existence. In summarizing this final novel in the cycle, Roth has offered the following:

> "In this third crime novel, I describe for the
> first time a woman as the main character who
> suffers following the death of her husband who fell

from the steps of a bridge. After his funeral, 'Lilli Kuck' spontaneously travels to Venice and traces the entries in a notebook that her husband wrote in mirror script, following his routes and trying to meet with the people he encountered during his final Venice sojourn. In so doing, she becomes more deeply involved in a dark mysterious crime case involving police murders that actually happened. In summary, her journey to Venice becomes a journey to herself, confronting the riddles of life itself. At the same time, the main characters from my first two Venice novels also make appearances . . ."[4]

Curiously, this is the first of Roth's many novels to feature a female protagonist; in addition, the novel is dedicated to his wife, Senta. In an interview, Roth confessed:

"I am married, have daughters and nieces, and am as interested in women as I am in men. At the outset I had to devote myself to other characters until I felt that I could risk writing about the inner life of a grieving widow."[5]

---

4 "Ich beschreibe in diesem dritten Kriminalroman erstmals eine Frau als Hauptfigur, die sehr unter dem Tod ihres Mannes leidet, der in Venedig über die Treppe einer Brücke gestürzt ist. 'Lilly Kuck' reist nach seiner Beerdigung spontan nach Venedig und folgt nach den Angaben aus einem Notizbuch, das ihr Mann in Spiegelschrift verfasst hat seinen Spuren und sucht jene Menschen, denen er bei seiner letzten Venedigreise begegnet ist. Dabei gerät sie immer tiefer in einen dunklen, mysteriösen Kriminalfall um Polizistenmorde, den man nachlesen kann. Insgesamt macht sie sich mit dieser Venedigreise auf die Reise zu sich selbst und begegnet den Rätseln um das Leben an sich. Dabei kommen auch die Hauptfiguren aus meinen ersten beiden Venedig-Bänden vor, . . ." From: Susanne Veronik, "Gerhard Roth: 'Es häufen sich Wunder über Wunder,'" in *meinbezirk. at/4521596*, 16 March 2021.
5 "Ich bin verheiratet, habe Töchter und Enkelinnen und interessiere mich für Frauen wie auch für Männer. Zuerst musste ich mich wohl selbst in anderen Figuren loswerden, bis ich den Eindruck gewann, ich

Like her male counterparts, Lilli Kuck is educated and professionally engaged in one of the fine arts (Michael Aldrian is in music, Emil Lanz in literature, and Lilli in the visual arts). She, too, is well-traveled, currently unattached (Aldrian is a divorcée, Lanz a widower, and Lilly, of course, a widow), and has a world view and temperament similar to those of her male predecessors: she is fearless, even reckless when challenged. Unlike the other two protagonists, however, Lilli is not forced to kill in order to survive—perhaps a concession to her femininity? Indeed, if we forgot her name, we could easily assume it is another of Roth's male characters. Strangely, Chapter 16, entitled "Lilli," has nothing to do with her. Perhaps, for Roth, men are not from Mars and women are not from Venus—both sexes are simply from earth, and thus indistinguishable, interchangeable?

In truth, this novel—substantially shorter than the first two male-dominated works—is also the weakest: the main character is not capable of carrying the action. Indeed, her possible witness to a nocturnal murder is flimsy: an experienced killer would either ignore her possible testimony or he would openly shoot to kill—a nudge into the Lagoon is hardly a death threat. So, the novel necessitates an unanticipated twist at the end, a *deus ex machina*—the return of Egon Blanc, the exposure and resolution of the conflict with his step-brother, and his resultant extravagant donations—which reveals the truth behind Klemens' death (fundamentally a case of mistaken identity) and allows others to forge new paths. Too, the "quick fix" at the end—Lilli's return to Vienna, Galli's rehabilitation, Riccardo's sudden retirement and escape to a city and country where he does not speak the language—is all too sudden, irrespective of the main characters' efforts, unfounded and, sadly, implausible.

---

könnte mich an das Innenleben einer trauernden Witwe wagen." Stefan Zavernik, "Es gibt keinen böseren Engel als die Liebe," *Kulturzeitung 80*, 11 March 2021.

Familiar Faces and "Endings"

> "At the same time, the main characters from my
> first two Venice novels also make appearances . . . ."

Each novel has characters from an earlier work in the cycle, perhaps on the fringes, but still connecting several works, if only superficially. Here, in the third novel, the main characters from the previous two works appear—making Venice seem less like a metropolis than a small town where everyone knows each other (and each other's business).

This final novel in the series basically updates the main characters in the previous two novels: the retired opera prompter and magician, Michael Aldrian; the literary translator, Emil Lanz; the former police Inspector Francesco Galli and his nemesis lawyer, Dr. Amanda Falchi; even the mysterious billionaire philanthropist Egon Blanc.[6] Indeed, the first two works even contain mention of the writer Philipp Artner, who originally appeared in *Grundriss eines Rätsels* (*Artner's Riddle*), and then as a neighbor in *Die Irrfahrt des Michael Aldrian* (*The Odyssey of Michael Aldrian*) and *Die Hölle ist leer—die Teufel sind alle hier* (*Hell is empty —And all the devils are here!*)

The reappearance of earlier characters is tied to Roth's vision of life and reality. At the termination of a challenge, the characters' lives go on, there is no conclusion, no finality; in Roth's novels,

---

6 Egon Blanc is a mysterious figure throughout the series. He and his wealth are, at crucial times, the fulcrum in people's lives. His life-changing generosity is appreciated, by and large, but the fact that Blanc so lavishly rewards people is somewhat suspect: Is he complicit in the dastardly deeds of his step-brother? Is his fortune earned through illicit businesses? Is he somehow related to the infamous Venetian mafia of the Mala del Brenta and its drug dealing? The novel generously compares Egon Blanc to a shogun whose samurai will kill for him or whose vassals (like the magician Aldrian and the translator Lanz) will carry out his harmless wishes. The shogun analogy is provocative and malleable.

there is no ending, no one lives "happily ever after." Thus we may re-establish contact and trace future developments of individual characters when they appear in subsequent works, again recognizing that change is not final, only temporary, as the future may bring further change(s).

There are no certainties, only possibilities: Galli, once scorned, is now rehabilitated, re-established with his sons, and introduced to his daughter-in-law; Lilli, threatened, is saved, and may return to her life and profession in Vienna; Riccardo, a police hero, resigns, drives to Vienna in Lilli's car, and intends to learn German. Both Lilli and Riccardo are unattached and available, the future is unknown, and life must go on. In the immortal words of the Mad Hatter: "Clean cup, move down!"

Love

"The most-evil angel is probably the involuntary separation of two lovers, especially due to death, in this case, of a perhaps unique husband."[7]

Love? Just a reminder: the six variations of love—from lust to simple pleasure—are, like beauty, in the eye (heart?) of the beholder. By definition an intrinsic human experience, love is subjective and thus unique. And the bases for love may be manifold:

---

7 Stefan Zavernik posed the question: "Ist der Titel Ihres neuen Buches als persönliche Erkenntnis zu verstehen? Und was erfährt man über die Liebe im Roman?" Roth's reply: "Der böseste Engel ist wohl der ungewollte Abschied von zwei sich Liebenden, vor allem der Tod, in diesem Fall eines wohl originellen Ehemannes." in: "Es gibt keinen böseren Engel als die Liebe," *Kulturzeitung 80*, 11 March 2021. Curiously, this description also fits the Guido Alberti family after his murder, though the aftereffects are not underscored in the novel.

physical appearance, interests or accomplishments, personality traits, compatibility or so-called "chemistry," among incalculable possibilities. While considered a durable human bond, it is also fragile, capable of flipping from passionate devotion to rejection and hatred in an instant.

Strangely, Lilli is inarticulate and unanalytical about her love for Klemens. At his funeral, she admits the mourners had no idea who he had really been. "She, herself, didn't even know" (p. 5). And that may be the true "mystery of life"—that we may not fully know the ones we love: Klemens withheld his work in progress, even going so far as to conceal its meaning by employing mirror script; Lilli also could not understand or tolerate certain violent aspects of his stories, preferring to overlook them. In Venice to investigate his mysterious death, she learns that he lied to her about his residence in Venice. She also discovers Klemens' secret reunions with his biological mother and father and brother which he had withheld from her. As evidence accumulates that he has been evasive, she begins to question their bonds. How can love withstand such deceit? Lanz, citing Shakespeare, offers an even more pessimistic view of relationships: "We are convinced that we understand other people, but that's a mistake. We don't even understand ourselves . . ." (112).

And her interest in Riccardo is also somewhat tenuous:

> "Riccardo resembled Klemens in appearance, but also in his behavior and interests, sometimes in weird ways. But he was more practical than Lilli's deceased husband. He couldn't draw particularly well, but when it came to telling a story, in retracing or anticipating events, they were like two peas in a pod" (179).

In addition to their similar appearance, behavior and interests as twins, Klemens depicted violence in his comic books, while Riccardo tracked down killers as a policeman. Is love transferable, under such circumstances? Lilli doesn't mention bonds other than their time together in a café. For his part, Riccardo provides a tangible commitment, in that he is willing to retire, move to Vienna, and attempt to learn German, since he doesn't speak Lilli's mother tongue.

An interesting analogy, as mentioned in the first novel and repeated here, posits that humans descended, not from apes, but from chameleons, emphasizing unanticipated changes, and not simply in coloration. How are individuals to anticipate, to recognize, to adjust? Both parties in a relationship may change, in unanticipated ways and at different rates.

While Lilli's love story is the basis for the plot, there is the equally compelling absence of love in Klemens' youth: after an illicit night, his biological father deserts the mother, and Klemens is unaware that he has a brother, Riccardo. Each member of the family is isolated and estranged from the lives of the others. Is this sadness, this loss of humanity, not the true "most-evil angel"?[8]

Love is but one important facet of life, yet another challenge to be recognized, enjoyed, surmounted or succumbed to. Yet another "labyrinth" in this thing called "life."

Conclusion—The Demonstrator

> "In summary, her journey to Venice becomes a
> journey to herself, confronting the riddles of life
> itself."

In Roth's fictional universe, life itself is the ultimate subject. He personally visits a foreign site, and like an experienced tour guide[9]

---

8 A similar instance of lost love concerns Egon Blanc and his step-brother, Jeremias Hainer, and their ill-fated battle for dominance.
9 Characters in several novels consider writing a personalized guide to their current locales—which is what Roth has already done on their behalf.

describes the profusion and diversity—geographical, cultural, historical, and personal, the preeminent as well as the deplorable. The abundance of experiences is a continuing theme, and each novel may contain one or more encounters with unique fields—for example, with viniculture, taxidermy, archaeology, hang-gliding, astronomy, falconry, botany, and apiculture to name but a few—a recurring feature in recent fiction by the autodidact, Roth.

Roth shows life to be a process, a continuum—as unpredictable as a *puzzle* or *riddle*, a *maze* or a *labyrinth*, to underscore recurring motifs in his recent fiction.

> "'Reality,' Lilli thought, 'is basically more complicated than any science and any religion. No one really knows their way around. Everything is always an attempt at an explanation.' She had always considered the two halves of her brain as labyrinths where thoughts strayed, and she felt as if she had been born into this maze of reality that no one understood . . ." (115).

A common thread in Roth's later novels is the extent and variety of life experiences. Through his fictional characters we encounter a foreign city, its structures, history, ambiance, etc. The translator Lanz, in *Hell is empty—And all the Devils are here!*, could represent all Roth's characters when the author proclaims:

> "The more closely Lanz looked, the more surprised he became that he had never paid any attention to the beauties of everyday life. But it was precisely things he had overlooked that now provided such wonders, he now realized . . . It was as if his

---

Moreover, Roth, as an avid and accomplished photographer—having published eight volumes of his own photos—uses his shots as reminders of the reality of the places he has visited and ultimately describes them in his fiction.

brain were trying to show him how the matter he had overlooked was actually a world unto itself" (108).

Roth has recently experienced serious health issues—a pulmonary embolism—and realizes how precious life is. As an admitted agnostic, he is not expecting salvation in some afterlife (and his characters share his conviction). All the more reason to appreciate and savor the here and now. It is, in Roth's opinion, all we have.

Moreover, the twenty-three illustrations interspersed throughout the three novels—ranging from classic art works to contemporary popular culture, including two facing photos featuring the natural beauty of tree leaves—visually highlight the variety and wealth of experiences, while the accompanying interpretations put each illustration in context and render them more familiar, more attainable. The most prominent illustration is that of Giovanni Tiepolo's *Il Mondo Nuovo*—a fresco stretched over two-pages of the novel. The demonstrator, according to Lilli is ". . . directing the thoughts of his audience . . .'" (160). The spectators, for their part, are starved for daydreams, prepared to be manipulated by these optical illusions, obsessed with the unknown, while they themselves stood at the verge of the ocean where ships were sailing to the New World or returning from that destination.

With little imagination, we could easily picture the writer, Gerhard Roth, in the role of the demonstrator, 'directing the thoughts of his audience.' His readership is curious about the unknown beyond their routines, while they stand on the brink of the world depicted in Roth's novels. The author is guiding us, from our safe and comfortable lives, to a world of complexity and wonder. He doesn't promise a smooth or happy ending to our lives, just a more in-depth appreciation of this world and its contents, including the enigma of its unanticipated twists and turns. To this end, one critic has concluded: "Ever since Roth has been writing, he has attempted to unravel human existence and the mystery of life itself. Has he succeeded? The answer is that there is no definitive answer…"[10] Each reader will have to decide for him- or herself, just as Gerhard Roth intends.

10   "Zeit seines Autorenlebens war Roth bestrebt, das Wesen des Menschen und das Rätsel des Lebens zu entziffern. Ob ihm das gelungen ist? Die Antwort ist, dass es keine Antwort gibt…" by dpa in: *Westfälische Nachrichten*, 23 June 2017.

The Author

Gerhard Roth (1942–2022) was born in Graz, the son of a medical doctor and a nurse. He originally intended to study medicine, but soon discontinued his studies. For ten years Roth worked as a computer programmer to support his growing family, but since the mid-1970s he was exclusively a writer. His major works consist of a cycle of seven novels, *Die Archive des Schweigens* (The Archives of Silence), and another novel cycle, *Orkus* (Hades). His work has earned extensive critical acclaim over the years, including the Döblin Prize (1983), the Kreisky Prize (2002), and the Grand Austrian State Prize (2016), among many others.

The Translator

Todd C. Hanlin (1941–2022) was Emeritus Professor of German at the University of Arkansas. He authored a book on Franz Kafka, edited Charles Sealsfield's *Austria as it is,* and a collection of essays entitled *Beyond Vienna: Contemporary Literature from the Austrian Provinces*; he wrote on numerous Austrian authors, translated a dozen novels and a similar number of plays, as well as a volume on *The Best of Austrian Science Fiction.* Hanlin translated six novels by Gerhard Roth, including the Venice trilogy, all for Ariadne Press.